"I'm gonna fix the both of you!" Honeywell bellowed, left index finger pointed at Charity and Bob from the end of his extended arm. "Go for your guns!"

Bob opened his coat to show he was unarmed. It appeared to mean nothing to Honeywell, who swung up his cocked Colt, ready to fire.

Charity drew her Colt Lightning from under her jacket and shot him in the gun arm. The five onlookers exchanged meaningful glances and hurried off. Charity stepped into the street, covering Honeywell with her double-action .38 Colt. She kicked his sixgun away and Bob retrieved it.

"You're wanted in Waco, El Paso and Amarillo, Honeywell. I'm taking you in to the sheriff."

With Bob backing her, Charity marched her prisoner to the corner and turned toward the sheriff's office a block away. They neared the alley that ran behind the saloon, when two gunnies stepped out into the thoroughfare, hands on the butts of their six-guns.

"Sorry, ma'am, but we can't let you take in our friend," one of the longriders informed her.

"You'll have to shoot me to stop it," Charity told him levelly.

In that instant Charity sent a .38 slug through the pelvis of one hardcase and followed by a bullet through the right ear of the other guy.

"Charity," Bob said in awe-filled voice. "I may not have taken what you said before entirely seriously, but I'm convinced now. You really are a bounty hunter. Not a scratch on you and you killed two and wounded one."

"That's not the nicest of compliments, but thanks anyway, Bob. Now let's get the sheriff. I still have work to do . . ."

E. J. HUNTER
THE AUTHOR OF <u>WHITE SQUAW!</u>

HEAD HUNTER

#2 TEXAS TUMBLE

ZEBRA BOOKS
KENSINGTON PUBLISHING CORP.

ZEBRA BOOKS

are published by

Kensington Publishing Corp.
475 Park Avenue South
New York, NY 10016

First printing: October 1987

Printed in the United States of America

Our special gratitude to Mark K. Roberts for his contribution to this book.

This volume in the adventures of Charity Rose is dedicted to Chief Beverly White Dove (*Coo-wee Coo-wee*) of our Cherokee People of Southern California. Belated congratulations on your April wedding.

—EJM

Chapter 1

Hot desert sun formed huge, sparkling diamonds on the surface of the clear rainwater, trapped in deep stone bowls. Deeply verdant algae slimed the rims of the basins and tadpoles darted frenetically about, in pursuit of those things important to tadpoles. Two cottonwoods, one tree tall, ancient and gnarled, the other a slender youth of some ten years, shaded a portion of the ground near the largest pond. Formed over the eons by the erosion of wind, water, and sand, this collection of natural catch basins had been given the name *los tanques* by the Spanish when they first arrived in the Southwest.

When the Americans came to what was now Arizona Territory, they didn't bother with a literal translation to *pond* or *swimming pool*. Rather, they somewhat lazily Anglicized the term into "the Tanks." So they had been called for as long as Charity Rose could remember.

Auburn-haired and lovely, Charity Rose lay on a thick blanket, spread under the limbs of the larger cottonwood. A slight breeze caused a dappled leaf pattern to move restlessly across her smooth, creamy, bare flesh. One well-shaped leg raised slightly, her eyes closed, she let her mind drift over the years, summoning the happy memories this special place conjured for her.

Long and soft, the fine, nearly white blond hair had floated around Corey Willis' head as the thirteen-year-old boy ran naked for the water. "L-let's g-g-g-et g-g-going, before I *explode!*" Corey had wailed in an intensity of embarrassment and quite real physical discomfort.

His words echoed in her mind. Behind him, a much younger Charity, equally unclothed, had squealed and raced after the lad. Corey was so brown and . . . and *beautiful*, Charity's contemporary reflection — like her thirteen-year-old mind and body had reacted — reminded her. Their adventure into swimming together in the nude had begun as a teasing challenge, escalated into a mutual dare and ended with each of them turning away from the other and shyly undressing under this same cottonwood.

Unable to restrain her rampant instincts, the youthful Charity had then commanded: "Well, turn around. Take a good look, and . . . and let me see you, too."

What she had seen made her knees weak and her belly squirm. That object, which had long been the subject of her curiosity and fascination, rose rigid and upcurved from a small delta at the junction of Corey's firm, muscular thighs. The sight of it only heightened the wild sensations that coursed through her young body.

"Well, ah," she had begun shyly. "Do you, ah, like me-me-me-meee?" the words reverberated through her adult memory.

"You're beautiful, did you know that?" Tom Thornton asked, shattering the impressions of the past. Solicitous, he added, "I'm sorry. Did I wake you?"

"No, Tom, dear," Charity responded, brushing

away a fluttering lock of her close-cropped auburn hair. "I was day dreaming, I'm afraid."

"About us, I hope?" the handsome young man, his rugged frame marred only by three puckered, purpled-centered scars on chest and abdomen, urged.

Charity flushed a pale pink and rose up slightly to kiss the gunshot wound near Tom's navel. An assassin's bullets had torn into Tom nearly two years before. Charity firmly believed she was the reason for Tom's near brush with death. She had been, and still was, the target of the killers, rustlers, and road agents who rode for an outlaw named Concho Bill Baudine. Baudine's men had murdered her father, the sheriff, during a jailbreak, raped her and left her shattered and abused beside his corpse. Charity believed Tom had gotten in the way of the vendetta she had sworn against the gang.

Rightly or wrongly, it had altered their relationship. She and Tom were to be married. At least, everyone in Dos Cabezas, Arizona Territory felt certain they would be. Now, with all that had passed since that terrible day when the Baudine gang rode in to free their leader, Charity still couldn't adjust herself to an "everything as usual" attitude.

She loved Tom. Really *loved* him. Yet, she found herself erecting barriers between them, even when she lacked material with which to construct them. She wanted to let go, give herself freely to life that might have been. Might have . . . if the bullets hadn't ripped apart her father and nearly destroyed the man she loved. Tom made it easier for Charity by stretching out beside her and taking her in his arms.

"Tell me about your day dreams," he murmured.

"Actually," Charity began reluctantly. "I was thinking about . . . about Corey and me. Our first time, right here in this very spot. We were . . . so young."

9

Undaunted by a rival from the past, Tom stroked her hair and kissed her under each sea-green eye. His breathing roughened and his caresses became more ardent.

"I know. Only thirteen, the both of you. You were a naughty girl."

"Yes. I suppose so. Only . . . it was so nice."

Fully aroused, Tom panted out. "And now? What about now?"

"That," Charity answered him, as she reached down and grasped his hardened flesh, "was nice. This is . . . *wonderful.*"

Slowly she slid his sensitive member down her taut belly, and into her moist womanhood. For a moment her heart lurched and memory made her recoil from the physical presence of a man, of the *threat* it seemed to imply. With a groan, Charity thrust the image from her mind and raised one leg, cocked it at the knee and let it drape over Tom's bare hip.

"Now, lover, now," she pleaded. "Quick, before . . . before I change my mind."

She groaned again as Tom entered her swiftly, drove to the hilt and then rested. Sunlight through the leaves highlighted the gold flecks in Charity's green eyes as she sighed in contentment and began a slow, circular motion with her hips, coupled with short back-and-forth jabs of her pelvis. She fixed her gaze on Tom's handsome, sweet face, his deep blue eyes, both arms now around his broad shoulders. Despite her fixed concentration, the features before her slowly dissolved into those of a befreckled, tow-headed boy of thirteen . . .

. . . Big, china-blue eyes wide with excitement, Corey Willis inexpertly and roughly drove his rigid, pulsing phallus back and forth. His eager, if inept, attentions gave young Charity shivers of delight. She locked her arms and legs around him and loudly encouraged him.

"Yes . . . more . . . more, Corey . . . Oh! Oh, Corey, Corey!"

Oblivion swallowed them in the same instant . . .

. . . *Oh, Corey, Corey!* a cold, disengaged portion of her mind mocked Charity. Corey was safe because Corey was years and miles away from here and now.

No! She wouldn't accept that. Never. She was here, where she wanted to be, with Tom, whom she loved with an aching desperation. Tom. It was Tom!

"Tommy! Oh, Tommy, Tommy, my love." Charity panted in a sudden fever.

Eagerly, Tom Thornton cooperated in the headlong rush to dissolution. He had carefully withheld himself, letting Charity arrange her feelings and physical needs in such a way as to insure there would be no more heartbreak, no last minute inability to release the pent-up emotions, and finally banish ghostly fears. Now as she called out to him he responded with all his heart.

Long minutes of loving went by in a blur. At last the final cascade of peak ecstasy engulfed them and they shuddered their way to peace and rest.

"We . . . we'll do that again," Charity remarked long moments later, her tone one of question and of promise.

"That . . . that we shall," Tom assured her.

How kind he'd been, Charity thought. So assured, patient and tender. Would life be like that always, if they were married? The shades of the past drew away, the happy ones content with her new happiness, the

11

bad images exiled by shared pleasure. *Mrs. Thomas Thornton*. It had a nice ring to it, Charity considered. No more nights alone on the desert, no more sick ache in her gut when she stalked down a vicious killer. No more fat reward payments, either. Nor the satisfaction of seeing the fear in the eyes of the cowards who had murdered her father. Mrs. Thomas Thornton. Charity Thornton. It did . . . have a wonderful appeal.

Megan Quincannon had come to the Promised Land in 1847, at the age of five. Famine plagued Ireland. Her parents, with five children, one on the way, managed to scrape together the passage. They settled in the coal country of Pennsylvania. There Megan, her sister Moira, and a total of seven other siblings grew up in conditions hardly better than those they had fled as tenant farmers for a brutal, absentee English landlord. Her father literally owed his soul to the company store. Their house, in a company town, was likewise beholden to the boss. To escape it all, Megan decided to follow her pre-pubescent urge to a vocation.

Shortly after her fourteenth birthday, barely into puberty, ignorant of almost everything in the world outside the coal fields, save the history of Holy Mother Church, she entered the convent as a novice. There she flourished in an atmosphere of care and rigid discipline. Moira, her younger sister by six years, later used another means to escape the horrible fate of coal town, or the equally—to her—undesirable one Megan had chosen.

Moira met, fell in love with, and eventually married a jovial, devil-may-care Irishman named Frank Patrick Michael Xavier Rose. Frank Rose took his bride away from the black grit, the damp cold, and the vile, sulphurous smoke of the coal fields. Barely fifteen at the time, Moira and Frank, who was twenty-three, lived an idyllic life for a year. Then Frank gave her a baby.

Never a robust woman, Moira weakened during pregnancy and took on a gaunt, hollow-cheeked visage that thoroughly frightened Frank Rose. How dearly he loved his fair *colleen*, and how boldly he had planned for their future. When she came to term, the baby was still-born. The doctor recommended a better climate than the streets of New York, say in the sunny fields of Iowa or Illinois. He also stated that Moira should refrain from having other children.

Within five months, Frank had her pregnant again, though both had been diligent in trying to avoid it. She died in childbirth. Moira, in her last year at the convent, left the novitiate and came to care for the new-born baby, whose father named her Charity Moira Rose. Frank sank into his grief. His love for Moira had been deep and total. He never remarried, moved the spinster aunt and infant girl west to Arizona and became a lawman. Megan, who disliked the isolation, the danger from marauding Apaches and *bandidos* from Mexico, thought the choice ill-fated. Frank's murder and the despoiling of her darling Charity verified her opinion.

Yet, she stayed on. Through the terrible year following Charity's "fate worse than death," she had prayed and given tender considerate care to the, to her, delicate young girl. She didn't see the hard edges Charity acquired, from years as a tomboy, and the determination for revenge. She did, however, come to back wholeheartedly Charity's plan for vengeance, when the Rose home was damaged by fire and her

13

own fire threatened by the Baudine gang. She listened patiently now, and with growing hope, as Charity bubbled on excitedly about how much she and Tom had rediscovered of their love for each other.

"Oh, Auntie Megan, I had a wonderful day. Tom was so considerate and kind, I . . . I felt guilty for the way I've put him off so long. He loves me, I know he does. And I . . . well, I *do* love him so. Now, maybe . . ."

The glow that radiated from Charity's unflawed complexion, which came from a long afternoon of satisfactory lovemaking, Aunt Megan Quincannon wrongly attributed to her improved outlook and greatly recovered health. She smiled approvingly and patted her niece's arm.

"Now, maybe ye'll be thinkin' of a home and kiddies runnin' around an' I'll be able to get about me own affairs," Megan suggested happily.

Charity arched a ruddy brow. "Oh-ho, it's 'affairs' ye'll be havin' is it?" she teased in a heavy, mock brogue. "An' what about yer vocation?"

A momentary flash of pain crossed Megan's face, then she brightened. "Oh, now, if I'd had a true vocation, I'd be Sister Simon Mary, or some such other now, and teachin' little uniformed brats in some school in New York. Such 'tiz not for the likes of a Quincannon, I fear. Though I've a desire to live in some place more hospitable than Dos Cabezas, I do."

"What? And not see your darling grand-nephews and nieces?" Charity teased. "You'd be knitting mufflers and caps and mittens for them and never seeing the dear wee ones."

Megan clapped her pudgy hands. "Ah, then, he popped the question, did he? Ye'll be Mrs. Thomas Thornton soon? When will Father Gomez read the

14

banns?"

"Well, I . . . er, we, ah . . . that is . . ."

A polite knock on the screen door to the kitchen saved Charity more discomfort at this interrogation. Through the distortions of the isinglass of the upper portion, Charity recognized the short, mustachioed figure of U.S. Marshal Noah Robinson. She came to her feet and crossed to answer his summons.

"Noah, come in," she said brightly as she swung the flimsy frame wide. A large cotton ball bobbed on its string, tied through the screen.

"Miss Charity, Miss Megan, good day to you," Noah Robinson declared heartily, twinkling eyes darting about in search of something into which he could expectorate a large blob of tobacco juice.

Bow-legged and slightly bent of back, the lawman crossed to the table with a rolling walk. There he took a chair, tipped back the wide brim of his 4-X Stetson and again sought a makeshift spittoon. Charity recognized the symptoms and produced a tall, empty, No. 6 peach can. Noah bobbed his head in thanks.

"Obliged." He spat a prodigious stream. "Now, if I could have a cup of water to wash it down? Then I think I'd enjoy some coffee."

"Ye'll be gettin' good Irish tea around this place, or nothin', Noah Robinson," Aunt Megan cautioned him with mock seriousness, small fists on her ample waist.

"Don't know if I'll be able to survive that, but I'm game to give it a try," Noah answered, teasing.

"What brings you here, Noah?" Charity inquired after her aunt had poured thick, white ceramic mugs of steaming brew.

"Well," the old time lawman began hesitatingly. "I hope I'm not the bearer of unwelcome tidings. Your,

15

er, exuberance made it impossible for me not to hear the talk of wedding bells as I approached the door," Noah added for explanation.

"That's all rather, ah, undecided," Charity hastened to straighten out. "What news do you have, Noah?"

"Well, Miss Charity, the word is that a certain Luther Waller, known as Lute and Wide-loop Lute Waller, is holed up near Las Vegas, New Mexico, with relatives of his in the Henry gang. That's Tom Henry."

Ice touched Charity's heart. *Lute Waller*. A grinning, jackal face, leering at her, bending over her already abused body and promising to come back for more some day. Lute Waller, who had shot her father in the chest, then the forehead.

"I . . . I'll make ready at once," Charity said in a cold, strangled voice. "That son of a bitch is going to pay."

"*Charity Moira!*" Aunt Megan exclaimed in horror. "Ye can't. Not now, *macushla*. Don't you see? Tom . . . young Tom's countin' on ye." Eyes wide with alarm, Megan could only wring her hands in the hem of her apron with trepidation.

"My father's ghost is counting on me, too," Charity answered shortly, like a voice from the grave. "I'll get my gear ready and leave in the morning. Are you coming with me, Noah?"

"I'd surely like to, Miss Charity. But it's outta my jurisdiction."

A small, pleased smile creased Charity's full, generous lips. "Then I'll do it alone."

Chapter 2

Warm, sweet and moist, a steady breeze blew up from the Gulf Coast to the southeast, drawn by high pressure over the East Texas savannah land. Rich fields of tall, green cane rippled in the moving air. Huge, anvil-headed clouds, with black bellies, built up far to the west, kept at bay by the same atmospheric cell. Two wagons made slow, often precarious passage along a rutted, slippery mud road. Two women and five children rode in the wagons, while their menfolk, clean-faced, with long, black hair, shoe-button eyes and high cheekbones, rode saddle mounts to the sides and rear of the little caravan. An occasional shrill whistle from one of the two pre-teen boys livened the draft animals and pierced the bird-song burdened air.

"This is gonna be easy," Westley Noonan snickered.

"Shut up, Wes," a hard, deep baritone voice commanded. "We don't want 'em gettin' any ideas until we come down on them," Concho Bill Baudine added.

Concho Bill, and six of his men, sat their horses in a tall stand of cattails along the creek that meandered roughly parallel to the roadway. They had been sent

17

there by the man who hired them, Dermott Wilkes, to "convince" the Perkins family not to move back to their summer place in the sugar cane fields of the Texas hills. Noonan might be right, Baudine considered, if all they had in mind doing was scare the moonshiners off.

Baudine, though, had his mind set on the contents of the wagons. White Injuns, that's what people in these parts called them. *Cha-roggies*, in the Texican dialect. Whatever they were, they had the reputation for taking everything they owned with them in their ubiquitous wagons. Most of them, common talk had it, possessed considerable wealth. Whatever the truth of that, they'd soon be finding out, Baudine acknowledged as he gigged his horse and rode out onto the muddy roadway.

Hand raised in the universal signal to halt, Baudine waited while the wagons rounded a low knoll and came into sight. The men, Concho Bill noted, instantly put hands to their weapons. Baudine tipped his hat with his left hand and formed his words into a friendly tone.

"You folks the, ah, Perkins family?" he inquired when the convoy drew near and stopped.

"We be," a large, barrel-chested man with a huge, hawk nose responded.

"Well then, it's good I found you. I, ah, have a little message of some importance from a well-intentioned friend. A, ah, Mister Dermott Wilkes."

"Dermott Wilkes ain't got a thing to say to us, Mister. An' we ain't got a word for him," the burly fellow with the big nose and long, jet hair growled. "Now, we'd be obliged if you'd move to the side an' let us pass."

"You didn't hear me clearly, Mister Perkins. I said Mister Wilkes has a message for you." Baudine's

18

voice had grown hard, cold and commanding. "He says you're to stay the hell outta this country. Your still and your moonshine business are his now."

Something low sounded in Bentbow Perkins' throat, like the warning snarl of a wolf. His left hand tightened on the buttstock of his rifle as he pulled it upward and free of the saddle scabbard. His black eyes became glowing chips of obsidian.

"You'd best tell Dermott Wilkes to have his land-grabbing sons of bitches clear of our ground by the time we get there, or we'll plant 'em under a new stand of paw-paw trees."

At a signal from Concho Bill, the six men accompanying him stepped their horses out onto the trail, at either side, weapons at the ready. Baudine nodded to them, a jaunty smile on his lips.

"Now, I'd say you just made a serious error, Mister Perkins. One might call it a fatal mistake."

At once the hardcases opened fire. They pumped round after round through their weapons, the slugs ripped and tore flesh and shredded clothing until the three adult males in the Perkins party reeled and swayed in their saddles and fell, their many wounds pouring blood. The women screamed and sought cover for themselves and their children, and the youngsters howled in terror. When the last dying man hit the ground, Baudine made a curt, slashing gesture with his empty left hand.

"Enough. Now, ladies, if you'll be so kind as to climb down out of those wagons?"

"You'll pay for this, you murdering scum," the older of the women responded in a hot, menacing tone.

"To the contrary, ladies. It's you who'll be paying, I regret to say. I want you and the children clear of the wagons by the count of three."

19

"If we don't?" the bolder, graying woman asked tightly, her hand reaching unseen for a shotgun.

"Then you'll join your menfolks. And be the cause of sending those sweet children along, too. *Now do it!*"

Sobbing, the younger woman obeyed Baudine immediately. She took along a toddler, wearing only a diaper, draped more like a breech cloth than a white man's garment. The older lady showed her face and looked at the younger in disgust. Then she shooed a boy of ten or so out of her wagon.

"Come on out of that wagon, Jimmy," she called to another lad of nearly the same age.

"Awh, Grammaw," the youngster complained.

Jimmy climbed out anyway, mud squished between his bare toes when he reached the ground. He rammed his hands into the pockets of his bib overalls. His shirtless upper torso had a light, coppery tan. Dark auburn hair, in a single braid, hung down his back. He glowered at the hard-faced killers.

"Now you, Grammaw," Baudine commanded in a mocking tone.

"You can go to hell, Mister."

Baudine's eyes narrowed. "Now, Grammaw, I don't want to kill you. Be a good girl and do like I say."

For a long moment they eyed each other. Then, with a sigh of resignation, Eula Perkins let the shotgun clatter back into the corner of the wagon box, climbed over the mud board and stepped gracefully onto the ground, her dress hem held high to prevent it soiling.

"All right, boys. Get those wagons rolling. While they're doing that, ladies, I'd appreciate it if you were to empty up all the valuables you and the children might be carrying."

"Devil take you, you're nothing but a common

thief," Eula snapped. "Dermott Wilkes has sunk mighty low to hire the likes of you."

Baudine gave her a light laugh. "It gets the job done, Grammaw. That's all that counts."

Despite Aunt Megan Quincannon's protestations, Charity Rose whistled up Butch, her gray and black half-wolf companion, saddled Lucifer and rode the coal-black gelding the three short blocks to the center of Dos Cabezas. She had a dual purpose in that.

First she wanted to inform Mark McDade, who had won the recent election and become sheriff in her father's place, and to get from him the necessary wanted poster and letters of introduction to enable her to hunt down Lute Waller. Also she needed to stock up on ammunition and reliable food for the trail. Charity found the main street of Dos Cabezas filled with more than the usual crowd. She worked her way through the throng of wagons and mounted visitors and stopped at the tie-rail outside the sheriff's office. As she crossed the boardwalk, she heard raised voices from inside and thought with a pang of when her father had held the position.

"I don't give a dang what might offend him," Mark McDade's tenor voice declared flatly. "Tell him that he's going to abide by what I say or face the consequences."

"Yes, Sheriff, but Mister McReedy is a . . ."

"Mister Brian McReedy," Mark interrupted the small, nervous-looking young attorney, "is going to come in here and answer for his son's outrageous behavior and criminal pranks, or I'll take that little bastard, Liam McReedy, on foot and kick his ass all the way from here to the ranch. I'm tired of having a thirteen-year-old, ill-bred, piss-ant bully breaking windows, setting fires and terrorizing all the children in town every day when he's supposed to be in school, doing his lessons."

"M-Mister McReedy isn't going to like this . . ."

"His likes are no concern of mine. He's going to corral that little monster, or I'm gonna lock up that—ah, hello, Charity," Mark amended as she opened the door and stepped in.

"Hello, Mark," she replied sweetly, giving no sign she had heard the heated discussion. "Oh, excuse me, are you busy?"

"No. Not at all. I don't believe you two have met. Charity this is Mister Ransom Hadley, attorney for Mister Brian McReedy. He's new in Dos Cabezas. Mister Hadley, Miss Charity Rose."

"How-do-you-do?" Hadley spit out indifferently, then gave her a cold fish hand to shake.

"Mister Hadley. Oh, Mark, would you like for me to have a little talk with dear Liam McReedy?"

"Indeed, Miss Rose?" Hadley interrupted rudely. "Precisely what would you tell the unfortunately misunderstood child?"

Beaming her best *gotcha!* smile, Charity told him. "I'd inform him that if he didn't start behaving himself, I would gladly take him by his scrawny little neck and wring it like a chicken."

"Oh, my, oh, dear me. Mister McReedy would definitely not like that."

"I'm sure he wouldn't," Charity went on, her anger roused. "If the 'unfortunately misunderstood child' sets another house afire in this community, I, for one, would gladly volunteer to put a bullet right between his eyes."

"Oh, dear. Oh, dear, dear me. *Violence* is never the answer." Hadley's small, close-set eyes narrowed in nasty speculation. "You are, I suppose, employed at the local, ah, saloon, Miss Rose?"

"Miss Charity's the daughter of the former sheriff. She's also a professional bounty hunter," Mark supplied gleefully, disgusted with this sissy lawyer from New York.

"Ah . . . oh, gracious me," Hadley dithered. "Hardly the sort to be imposed upon the tender minds of our children."

"If you *had* a child," Charity bore in, sensing the odd aspect in the aura of the little lawyer, "*he'd* probably wear dresses and play with dolls."

"See here, Miss Rose, this is not the time for personal insults. Now, as to Liam McReedy . . ."

"Liam McReedy is a nasty little brat," Charity told him coldly and precisely, "who should have been strangled at birth. If Brian McReedy has sunk to hiring the likes of you to weasel his son out of his criminal acts, then it's about time we gave serious thought to a large vat of tar and a number of feather pillows," she concluded hotly, then turned her attention to Mark McDade. "Though I really would like to get a good look at Liam, Mark. If he doesn't mend his ways he'll be showing up on a wanted poster before very long and it would give me the greatest of pleasure to get paid for bringing him in."

"Y-you're—you're barbarous, the both of you!" Hadley gasped.

"No, my dog, Butch, is barbarous," Charity informed him. "He gnaws on people, I do not."

At the side of Mark's desk, Butch looked up brightly at the sound of his name and exposed a plentiful set of large, healthy teeth. Ransom Hadley paled. He rose hastily, fumbled on a derby hat and made quickly for the door.

"Don't forget what I told you, Mister Hadley. I want Brian McReedy in here to pay for every cent of damage his son did so far, I want him to publicly spank that little bastard and I want that kid in this jail every weekend for the next six months."

"I — I — I'll get a court order to stop such cruel and unusual punishment," Hadley threatened as he hurried out onto the boardwalk, one hand clutching his derby the other the doorknob.

"Fuck your court order, Hadley," Mark yelled after him. "Uh, sorry, Charity."

Charity grinned at him. "I couldn't have said it better myself."

"What brings you to town?"

"I'm off to get Lew Waller. He's supposed to be with the Henry gang over around Las Vegas, New Mexico."

"And you've just got to go bring him in?"

"You've got it, Mark."

Ignoring the obvious invitation to the never-ending argument, Mark resigned to the inevitable. "When are you leaving?"

"Tomorrow, after church."

"Ummmm. You know I worry about you, traveling alone and all."

"And I appreciate it, Mark. Even so, I'm going." Then, to change the subject, she inquired, "Say, what's all the excitement in town about?"

"Oh, didn't you hear? There's a family of itinerant preachers come to Dos Cabezas. They've scheduled a revival meeting at the saloon for this evening. Supposed to be some powerful preaching. It'll be followed by a hoe-down, so wear your fancy squaw dress."

Charity frowned. "Do you think I should go, Mark?"

"Why not? In fact, why not come with me? You love to dance."

"Well, there's Tom, of course. But, what I mean, these, ah, evangelists, have their own brand of religion. Do you think Father Gomez would approve?"

"Why not? The times they are a-changing."

Yes, indeed, Charity thought. The times were changing. Few people now recalled that her own church, to which nearly everyone in and around Dos Cabezas had gone for generations, had been established as a mission church nearly two hundred years before. Designed to tend to the needs of the Indians and Spanish population, it had slid into disrepair and been nearly abandoned by the time a handful of Irish Catholics settled in the town during a brief mining boom. For a while that strengthened the parish. New settlers, finding no other church, opted for the Roman rite as better than being without religion at all, and it became habitual.

Now, her reflections continued, with easier and safer travel through these parts, other faiths will naturally come around. They, too, might make their mark, or be absorbed by the timeless hills and desert and the eternal Church of Rome. Who could tell if that would be for the good or not? Her warm smile eased the frown away.

"You're right, Mark. It sounds like fun. I'll go with you. And I promise, I'll dance your legs off."

Chapter 3

Even the cobwebs—heavy with smoke residue and dust—had been brushed off the open beams, the *viegas* ceiling swept clean, new sawdust put down, and every kerosene lamp and reflector-backed candle burned brightly. Oldtimers around Dos Cabezas swore that they'd never seen the Idle Time Saloon looking so spic and span. Red-white-and-blue bunting—usually displayed only on the Fourth of July—had been broken out and hung along the backbar. A small lectern, which had come from the evangelist's wagon, stood dead-center in front of the mahogany bar, which was situated to the left of the batwing entrance in the traditional manner, and a large, plain cross had been set on the blue marble top in back of that. Charity Rose and Mark McDade sat in sturdy captain's chairs near the back. The crowd, though not overly large, seemed satisfactory enough.

A number of local wags held it privately that, had it not been for the hoedown, there wouldn't have been half the number who elbowed their way into the liquor emporium. The local chapter of the Women's Christian Temperance Union, all five of them, held a prominent spot right up front, on the far left. Their high button, ebon shoes, black dresses, hats and veils, might have been a uniform. The small placards they carried on lengths of broom handle advertised their cause.

DOWN WITH DEMON RUM!

That not one in ten of the others present agreed with them daunted them not at all. They sang lustily—the only time they lusted about anything, the wags said—when the piano struck up the familiar chords of a hymn. Eyes bright with their zeal, they easily segued from *When the Roll is Called up Yonder*, to *The Old Rugged Cross. Onward Christian Soldiers* nearly put them into a frenzy.

Which caused Ab Dillingham, the new proprietor of the Idle Time, to fidget and have horrible visions of hand axes in the possession of these hard-faced ladies, wreaking terrible destruction on his stock in trade. At last a tall, cadaverous gentleman in a long, black frock coat strode from the saloon office—which had been used as a temporary vestry—and took his place behind the lectern.

His long, thick shock of white hair gave his horsey face a leonine aspect. Burning blue eyes, alight with the Word, moved right-left-right, taking in the congregation of Dos Cabezas. He remained quiet, hands clasped in an attitude of prayer, until the assortment of gamblers, soiled doves, bar flies, gentry and cowboys became silent. Then, in a sonorous voice which could have rattled stained glass windows, had there been any, he offered the opening prayer.

After that, the preaching came hot and heavy. He paused after some fifteen minutes, while the gathering sang *Rock of Ages*. While the discordant harmony filled the air, a rather plain, dumpy-looking young woman and a stout matron with gray hair in a tight bun, covered by a lace veil, passed among the throng with velvet bags, stretched on hoops at the

27

ends of long poles.

With occasional promptings from the evangelist, such as, "Give generously unto the Lord, and He shall reward you manyfold," the offering was collected. Beaming, the WCTU ladies believed with beatitude, the cynics considered the size of the collection to be more the cause, the preacher started in again.

"We often hear about the benefit of being Saved. I'm sure other ministers of the Gospel have told you about being redeemed in the Blood. Yet, how often do we get the opportunity to see the results of this awesome gift of Love? Brother Smith here," he made a wide, sweeping gesture toward a young man, dressed as he was with white shirt and black string tie, who stood in the open doorway to the office. "Brother Smith was the blackest of sinners when first I met him. He was not a stranger to any evil. Yet he came to know the Lord and to love Him as I do, as does my dear wife and daughter. And, yes, he eventually washed himself in the Blood of the Lamb and became . . . my son-in-law. Praise Him, all you people! You see before you the living product of the Lord's Love! Hallelujah! I want . . . I want Brother Smith to come up here and tell you good folks what it's like to live in sin. I want him to tell you what it's like to die a little every day and to believe there is no way to help yourself. Come on, Brother Smith. Come Witness for the Lord!"

Amid indecorous applause and a few shrill whistles and catcalls, Brother Orin Smith marched to the pulpit and assumed the position held by his father-in-law. He raise both arms above and called for silence. Then he began to give his testimony.

When he finished, there was not a dry eye among the ladies of the WCTU, nor, for that matter, among the soiled doves. Charity and Mark exchanged amused glances.

"He really knows how to wring them out," Mark said in *sotto voce*.

"Mark! You're really awful, do you know that?" Charity responded in like tone.

"What would good Father Gomez say?" Mark teased.

"Harrumph!" Charity sat with arms folded, a mock pout on her lovely lips.

Once again, the Reverend Tom Uzzel took over and began his harangue that was guaranteed to bring the sinners down the aisle to repent. He scattered about generous portions of fire and brimstone and spoke darkly of the terrible fate that awaited all who did not heed the Call. As he swept into his finale, he touched the souls of two ladies of the evening and a gambler who had been down on his luck of late. Heads bowed, they trooped to the front and knelt before the lectern.

Old Tom did some powerful praying over them, clamped their heads in a grip that would have opened the jaw of the stubbornest mule, and pronounced them Born Again. After the closing hymn, he raised his hands far above his head and made an announcement in his "voice of doom."

"Now, folks, with the Glory of the Lord all around us, we come to the less serious part of our evening together. Our hoedown music will be played by Jesse Ortiz and Shamus O'Toole on fiddle, Ramon Garcia and Hector Beltran on guitar and Vinny Mallory on the concertina. There's punch and cookies from the dear ladies of the WCTU and lots of coffee, courtesy of Mister Dillingham, proprietor of this establishment. After that . . . after that . . ." his zealous oratory dwindled. "After that, it'll be business as

29

usual," Uzzel concluded in a near-murmur.

Music struck up, an odd mixture of *vaquero corriadas*, Irish sea chanties and contemporary polka and waltz. Mark took Charity by the hand and led her to the hastily cleared area in the center of the floor. He took her in his arms, careful to hold her a respectable distance from him, and they spun around the clapping, stamping onlookers. Others joined them.

"Oh, Mark, this is delightful," Charity exclaimed as his energy, if not precisely his style, spun her toward dizziness.

"I like the company, too," Mark suggested.

"Flatterer," Charity riposted.

When the second number ended, they stopped, breathless, and Mark led Charity to where the evangelists stood to one side. Charity thought the ministers watched the revelers with slight disapproval. Mark hurried to make introductions.

"Reverend Uzzel."

"Good evening, Sheriff."

"Reverend Uzzel, Mrs. Uzzel, Brother Smith, Sister Smith, may I present Charity Rose."

Rev. Uzzel, splendid in his patriarchal garb, glowed. "A good evening to you, Sister Rose, and the blessings of the Lord."

Brother Orin Smith all but slobbered. "You're a very lovely lady, Sister Rose," he blurted as he attempted to take Charity's hand and kiss it.

Mrs. Uzzel beamed, Sister Smith glowered.

"Thank you all, it's a pleasure to meet you. Ah, however, I'm not one of your persuasion and so it's not 'Sister' Rose. I have an aunt who was going to be a nun, 'Sister Simon Mary' as she puts it, but I'm just Charity."

Slight frowns creased the Uzzels' foreheads. Deborah glared open hatred and contempt. "You're of the Roman faith, I take it," Deborah spat, in a tone to imply she might have said, "You're from the bottom of an outhouse."

"Why, yes," Charity returned easily, free of guile. "Nearly everyone here is. Didn't you know that?"

"Ah-hem," Rev. Uzzel gently injected. "That's neither here nor there, Daughter. They're all children of Gawd."

"Pagans is what they are. Idolators, worshippers of . . ."

"*That* will be quite enough, Daughter. Ask Gawd's forgiveness and treat our gracious company with due respect," Tom Uzzel ground out.

"I'm not under your . . ." Deborah began angrily, then turned away, to cast an imploring glance at her husband.

"Brother Tom is quite right, Deborah," Orin Smith admonished his wife. "We should do our best to be kind to our new friends." He flashed Charity a toothy smile.

"Ah, Charity, I thought you might take particular interest in meeting the Uzzels."

"Why is that, Mark?"

"As it happens, the Uzzels are taking their revival eastward. They intend to stop in Las Vegas, on their way across New Mexico Territory and into Texas."

Eyes turned jade-green and locked hard on Mark's. "My, what a coincidence," Charity observed with mild sarcasm. "As it happens, I'm on my way there tomorrow," she went on to inform the evangelists.

"I see the workings of Gawd's hand in this," Tom Uzzel declared.

Beyond them the music segued into a nearly expert rendition of a popular *Passo Doble*, the Mexican polka. Whoops and hollers came from the dancers

31

and spectators alike when a snare and bass drum came from behind the piano and someone substituted a big clay jug for the tuba. Little Timmy Jordan returned breathlessly to the saloon with his silver cornet and caught up the notes with ease. Why not, Charity considered. His instructor on the horn, the only music teacher in Dos Cabezas for that matter, was Amordios Calderon.

"What is that awful noise?" Deborah asked with distaste.

"That's the Mexican Two Step," Charity delighted in telling her. "*Everyone* does it."

Old Tom Uzzel cocked a shaggy, white brow. "Anything like the Mississippi Two Step?"

"I don't think so," Charity replied with a look of innocence.

Then her natural bent for mischief came to the fore. She looked directly at Deborah and spoke slowly. "Though I imagine any number of those who deserved it have been hanged to the tune of *El Costeno*."

Mark kicked her lightly in the shin. "Charity!"

"I *am* being nice, Mark," Charity told him under the racket of the music. "Nice as I can, at least."

"I'd hoped you'd get along with them," Mark offered, a note of disappointment tingeing his words.

Charity suspected she knew full well the reason. "I am. At least as well as I need to."

"Tell me, Miss Charity," Rev. Uzzel interrupted their private discussion. "Do you know much about Las Vegas?"

"It's a rough town, Reverend. There are cattle barons, cowboys, rustlers, wide-loopers and road agents in Las Vegas," Charity informed him.

Old Tom nodded gravely. "Yes, I've heard of the doin's in Las Vegas. In particular of the activities of a ne'er-do-well called Hoo Doo Brown."

"Hoo Doo Brown, Reverend, is none other than Justice of the Peace, Henry G. Neil. He runs the entire illegal activities in Las Vegas from his comfortable office, where he also dispenses justice. Or what there is of it in that town."

"I wasn't aware of that, Miss Charity. It makes no difference, though," Uzzel declared, pointing a long, admonitory finger toward heaven. "For I am strong in the armor of the Lord. I'll convert Justice Neil's soiled doves and gamblers, save the souls of the dispensers of spirits, and bring to redemption the outlaws." Old Tom brushed back his coat and affectionately patted the well-worn butt-stock of a Colt revolver. "Then I shall run the notorious Hoo Doo Brown out of town on a rail."

"That's an ambitious undertaking, Reverend," Charity allowed drolly. Noticing Mark's continued agitation, Charity suspected even more his motive in the introduction. The reverend's next words convinced her.

"Since we're all bound for the same destination," Old Tom intoned like an announcement from the pulpit, "it would seem Gawd's will that we all travel together. We would be most pleased, and greatly relieved, considering the dangers that could befall a young woman alone, if you could consent to accompany us."

"Well, I . . ." Charity captured the expression on Mark's face. "Why, thank you, Reverend Uzzel. I would appreciate that very much."

Mark McDade beamed, proud of himself for the clever manner in which he had arranged to insure Charity's safety. For his own part, Rev. Uzzel exhibited considerable pleasure in obtaining the company of a beautiful young woman. He, and his wife, he admitted secretly, were immensely flattered by it.

Although, he considered, his daughter would be furious. Deborah had always been the jealous and possessive type. Even as a child with her dolls. Coming to Jesus had done little to temper her self-generated outrage. Their journey could be a bumpy one. In spite of it all, he smiled broadly and gave Charity a fatherly pat on one shoulder. The music struck up again and Orin Smith took Charity's hand without asking.

"Thank you, no," she told him coldly. "I always make it a point to dance with 'the man what brung me.' "

Oily as a shedding snake, Orin turned not a hair, but addressed himself to Mark. "May I have the pleasure of a dance with your lovely escort?"

Matching insincere smiles, Mark half-bowed and leaned close to Orin, then whispered in his ear, "Fuck off."

Of those present, only Charity's keen ears picked up his words. They sent her into a fit of giggles. Unaware of what had transpired, Deborah, returning to the group, saw only that her lecherous husband had the hungers for Charity and that the snotty young slip of a girl held him in abject contempt. Rage kindled in her stomach and began to smolder. When Orin flushed red, following Mark's remark and let go of Charity's hand, Deborah grew angrier. Nodding to the Uzzels, Charity and Mark spun out onto the floor and moved gracefully into the rhythm of a waltz.

"We're *not* taking *her* along, are we, Father?" Deborah wasted no time in snapping at her parent.

"Certainly we are. This is hardly the country for a young woman to be traveling about without an escort."

"She's a papist!" Deborah hissed. "She's a coarse, vulgar hussy, and a man trap."

"Quite the contrary," Old Tom assured her, having observed Charity's reaction to Orin Smith. "She is a lady of considerable quality and good taste."

"I saw what went on between her and Orin. I'm going out there and slap her slutty face."

"No . . . you're . . . not!" Tom Uzzel's words had a sepulchral tone.

His admonition had no time to take effect on his daughter, as a stir at the main entrance announced the arrival of the Thornton family. Young Tom, still using a cane, trailed his parents, escorting his younger sister on his arm. A moment later, another stir came when Abe Winkler stormed through the batwings.

Winkler, an unkempt, loutish tippler who lounged about the saloons and hauled firewood for the town when in need of funds, had a reputation as a bully and a coward. A few stiff shots of pop-skull made him a tiger, though. When in his cups, few would wish to cross him. Now he stood, swaying, eyes bloodshot, the stench of whiskey wafting from him in heady waves. He raised a grubby, crack-nailed finger and pointed at Tom Thornton.

"There you are, you fancy-pantsed sissy. Hide behind that cane and a phony limp, will you? Turn around here and fight me like a man."

Contrary to the circumstances described in multitudes of dime novels, the cattlemen, cowhands and drovers did not indulge themselves in orgies of fisticuffs. More directly, and permanently, they settled their differences with firearms or knives. Consequently, Tom Thornton thought himself challenged to a gunfight.

"I'm not armed, Abe," Tom responded, his back

35

still to his tormentor. "You'd best pick another time."

Winkler reeled forward, drunk, but not beyond the point of viciousness and controlled brutality, and slammed a sneak blow into the back of Tom's neck, slightly above his shoulder blades. Tom stumbled forward, into his father, and toppled to one side.

Abe came on, using his feet. He kicked Tom in the thigh and shouted wildly, spittle flying. "I know you got a hold out, you yellow-belly. Draw it, you bastard! Draw!"

From seemingly nowhere, Mark McDade appeared at Abe Winkler's side. Right hand on the smooth grips of his Colt, Mark used the other to grab Abe's gunhand.

"Hold it right there, Winkler. He said he was unarmed. You're gonna sleep it off in jail."

"Like hell I will, Sheriff. I'm gonna make this lump of dung pay for what he did."

"What is it he's done to you?" Mark demanded.

"He dishonored my sister."

Such an accusation so startled Tom that, without thinking, he blurted out, "Bullshit."

Mark yanked Abe's wrist so hard he jerked the man around to face him. "Wise up, Abe. You know as well as I do that it could be any one of a dozen men who managed that. The only one I'm *sure* it couldn't be, is Tom Thornton."

Abe's eyes narrowed, grew meaner. "What do you mean by that?"

"I'd rather not say this in public."

"Go on, Sheriff," Abe taunted. "Let the whole world know."

"Tom and Charity are engaged. He's not likely to cheat on her. As to your sister, I'm sorry, Abe, but she's not exactly known for having taken a vow of celibacy," Mark replied coldly.

36

"She's only fourteen!" Abe raged. Then he turned his attention back to Tom. "I'm gonna kill him. So help me, I'm gonna kill him."

Mark violently shoved Abe from him. Then he followed with a hard left to Abe's jaw. Unseen by Mark, Abe's younger brother, Benny, slid a small pistol from under his loose-hanging shirt. He started the muzzle up to center on Mark's back when white-hot pain exploded in his wrist and the gun dropped from uncontrollable fingers.

Charity Rose, who held a small clasp knife, dripping blood, stood at Benny Winkler's side. She shook her head sadly. "That's not playing fair, Benny."

Benny started for her when a low, warning growl sounded near his legs. He looked down to see Butch, Charity's wolf-dog eyeing him, fangs bared in what Benny took to be happy anticipation of chewing on his flesh.

"Excuse us, folks," Mark McDade announced in a coaxing tone. "Only a small disturbance. Go on with the dancing. We've got it well in hand."

"Thanks, Mark," Tom Thornton said sincerely, coming up somewhat unsteadily from the floor. "I appreciate it. I really wasn't armed."

"I know it, Tom. And I know you'd not had anything to do with Jenny Winkler."

"I'm obliged, all the same. And, ah, you might give your thanks to Charity. She stopped Benny Winkler from back-shooting you."

Mark turned to Charity, eyes wide and filled with gratitude. He took her hands in his. "I knew there was some good reason I asked you to come with me tonight."

"Oh, Mark, I . . ." Charity's voice flagged and her jaw dropped slightly at the reaction she read on

Tom's face. "Oh, Tom, I . . ."

"Never mind," Tom snapped icily. "I understand completely."

He turned away and walked unevenly across the room to stand beside his parents, his back kept rigidly, and permanently, to Charity. Frigid fingers squeezed Charity's heart and her knees went weak. She turned an appealing look on Mark McDade, who, occupied with his prisoners, never let it register.

"Let's get these two down to jail. Doc Pritchert can patch Benny up and I'll let 'em go some time tomorrow," he said, all business.

Charity gave a backward glance. *Tom, oh, Tom,* she thought desperately.

Chapter 4

Cactus wrens chirped awake the morning. Pale bands of white, pink and pastel blue stretched the long, saw-toothed horizon to the east. Lucifer, his black coat shining, twitched impatiently while Charity saddled him. The heady scent of yesterday's sunbaked mesquite, sage and wild flowers perfumed the air. Butch, tail wagging for once, sat on his hind quarters, tongue lolling, while his bright gray-shot, black eyes studied his master's efforts.

Charity Rose, dressed in the costume of a young man, gave her closest companions much to puzzle over. She had been crying. The residue of her emotional aura could be smelled by horse and dog alike. It contributed to their restiveness. The early hour dimly reminded them of other times when such a departure meant a long adventure. Charity felt heartsick. She hadn't even time the previous night, certainly not this morning, to explain to Tom what had happened. His obvious hurt at seeing her escorted by Mark McDade speared her heart with sorrow. She *did* love Tom. Yet, at times, she still cringed from his touch. His lovemaking was wonderful. The best she'd ever enjoyed. Still, in the recesses of her mind she harbored the terrible ordeal which had so scarred her

39

being.

Resigned, Charity had to admit that her feelings for Tom were impossible to sort out. Traveling with the family of evangelists would hardly give her time to reconcile her jumbled emotions, she considered. Damn Mark McDade for arranging her convenient safe escort. She should have never told him about the Apaches who had attempted to raid her camp on her way to Santa Fe that time. She kneed Lucifer, a bit firmer than need be, and made the final yank and tie-off on the cinch. Time to be going. Aunt Megan sat in the kitchen, dabbing at her eyes with her apron hem, Charity knew.

It would mean another scene, but she went back anyway. "It's important, Auntie Megan, don't you see? He's all but flaunting himself as though nothing could ever happen."

"Who?"

"Lute Waller, of course, Auntie. No one else will arrest him. Particularly over in Las Vegas, with Hoo Doo Brown calling the shots. I *have* to go."

"I'll light a candle ev'er day far ye. And pray. Oh, 'tiz a regretful thing it is."

"Let's not go into that. Kiss me good-bye. I have to join up with the Uzzels."

"Heretics, they are, the lot of 'em. An' me poor Charity Moira goin' off with 'em as eats babies far their heathenish practices they do."

"Oh, poo. You know better than that," Charity chided.

Megan gave her a wink. "Sure an' they say the same about us. So 'tiz but a little tit-for-tat. Don't be takin' risks, *macushla*. Come home safe and sound. And may God go with ye."

40

Two high-sided, top-heavy wagons with sturdy, thick wheels, waited at the far side of the livery, where old Tom Uzzel had made camp. The minister sat in the driver's seat of the lead one, his wife beside him. Deborah Smith drove the second rig, with Orin on horseback. Reverend Uzzel and Brother Smith greeted Charity warmly, Mrs. Uzzel indifferently, and Deborah coldly. Old Tom cracked his whip and the small cavalcade moved out.

They had hardly started when Charity recognized the whiney, complaining voice of Deborah, her scathing remarks directed to her roving-eyed husband. "Dressed like a man, she is. It's scandalous. Obscene."

"Now, Deborah. Where's your Christian charity?"

"Not wasted on the likes of that, I assure you," Deborah snapped. "You're a fine one to talk. 'Good morning, Miss Charity. It's a beautiful day, isn't it?' " Deborah mocked his earlier greeting. "She's a witch, I tell you, with her cap set to steal you away to the devil."

"Bosh."

"What?" Deborah demanded in a strangled note.

"Bosh. I said, 'bosh.' And poppycock, too."

"You wait and see. You wait," Deborah wailed.

Charity rode ahead a way, scouting the countryside. By ten o'clock, she estimated, it would be an inferno on the high plateau. Too bad they couldn't make good enough time to slip down into the shady canyon that wended northeastward from Dos Cabezas. She wondered how the draft animals, which didn't seem to receive the best of care, managed so long in the desert. Near the noon hour, Charity stopped at a place shaded by mimosa and tall mesquite bushes. The wagons arrived a short while later.

Throughout the meal of cold chicken, yesterday's

41

bread and left-over beans, Deborah complained about the food. She also took the desert in general to task. A short distance away stood a large smoke tree. The breeze, dancing through its delicate leaves, created a spectacle of beauty and serenity. Charity fixed her attention on it and wished Deborah could give off her hating for a while, at least long enough to appreciate the glory that surrounded her. When one of the jealous young woman's barbs flew her way, Charity remained oblivious of it until old Tom's sharp, strangled retort pierced her consciousness.

"For shame, Deborah!" he declared like a thunderclap. "Unseemly speech like that is an abomination before the Lord. You will apologize at once."

"No. I will not."

Tom's sharp slap focused Charity's attention on the lamentable scene. Why, she wondered, didn't Tom Uzzel leave Deborah's disciplining to her husband? Tom's next words enlightened Charity on that subject.

"Why don't you curb that woman's tongue, Brother Orin?" old Tom demanded in an interrogatory manner. "Woman is a creature of sin and must be commanded by her husband. It says that in the Book somewhere. Is it that you possibly see our young guest in the same light as Deborah does?"

"Oh, ah, no, sir. Not in the least, Brother Tom. Not at all," Orin replied hastily, his eyes seeking Charity.

"Well, the food isn't the best," Matilda Uzzel came in late in the discussion. "It would be nice to have some fresh meat."

Tired of being bathed in the green light of Deborah's jeaousy and resentment, Charity decided to evade that acid tongue by responding to the needs of Mrs. Uzzel. She gathered up rifle and kit, called to

Butch and they started out with Lucifer to do a bit of hunting. At least she would pay her way. And, perhaps, some fresh meat would sweeten Deborah's stomach and thus her disposition.

Half an hour ride brought Charity to a small seep spring she knew well. Wild creatures gathered here to slake their large desert thirsts. She picked her location well and leaned back to await something of interest. Made drowsy by the heat and lack of breeze, Charity's mind slowly slid backward over the few short years of her life . . .

. . . She had been three years old when her father started for Arizona. With all their possessions in the wagon, consisting of only those objects readily portable, they had little with which to make a new life when they arrived in Havupai County, Arizona Territory. Neighbors gifted the newcomers with many items, including clothing for a small child. Among them had been moccasins and britches in the Indian style.

Charity had taken to them. Through no conscious fault, her father had raised her as the son he never had. She loved that, too. She learned to ride astride of her mount, to hunt, shoot, fish and clean the game she took. She went swimming at the Tanks, which eventually led to the wonderful discoveries she encountered with Corey Willis, and even got into an occasional fistfight. By the age of eight, the respectable ladies of Dos Cabezas declared her an irretrievable tomboy. The explosive blossoming of her sexualty ended all that.

By fourteen, Charity thought of nothing save dresses, bows, dances and parties. And, of course, of Corey. For nearly two years they shared their pleasure

43

and passion. Good fortune smiled on them; for never did an accident occur that would have shattered their secret paradise. Stirred by the direction of her reflections, Charity wondered idly where Corey might be at that very moment. Would he be a rancher, like his father? Or a soldier? Perhaps a lawman?

He never tired of going into town and hanging around the sheriff's office, listening raptly to stories of outlaws and their capture. With a sudden, aching pang, Charity realized how terribly much she missed Corey Willis, with his soft, white hair, crooked line of freckles over his high cheeks and nose, and the gap between his front teeth. He wouldn't look like that now, she realized with regret. Time would have changed him. It certainly had her . . .

. . . With a start, Charity realized that a perfect target stood poised at the water's edge, as though waiting for her. She slowly raised her rifle into position and gently squeezed the trigger.

Proudly, Charity returned to the wagons with the dressed-out carcass of a fat, wild burro. She waved friendly greetings and hove to when she saw Tom Uzzel intended to make camp for the night. When he saw her offering he waxed eloquent in praise.

"Thunderation! Why, that's the nicest burro I've seen in a long time. Makes my mouth water. What say we disjoint it quick like and take that rack of nice, fat ribs to broil over the fire?"

"I've been thinking about that all the way back," Charity informed him.

"Burro!" Deborah shrieked upon sight of the skinned carcasses. "How *ghastly!* I won't . . . I absolutely can't, can't, can't eat that repulsive thing." Faking an excellent sob of desperation, she flung

herself away and ran for the wagon.

Utterly astonished by his daughter's reaction, old Tom could only rise from his stooped position and watch after her. Then he enlightened Charity. "Tarnation, I can't see what got into that gal. Why, she was *raised up* on burro meat. Most not near so prime as this. Think she could be puttin' on airs, Maw?" he inquired of his patiently suffering wife.

"That's, or she's in the family way," Matilda Uzzel responded shortly.

"Not much chance of that," Orin Smith grumbled. "Considerin' the way she sees such things, it'd take a second performance by the Holy Ghost to get her caught."

"Don't blaspheme," Matilda snapped.

Tom Uzzel had to resort to the ploy of a coughing spell to mask his chuckles. That son-in-law of his might be a dunderhead, but he sure knew well how to make his point.

Rattling along over the bumps and ridges, the stage out of Las Vegas for Santa Fe and points south raised a tall column of ochre. Its next stop, shortly before dark, lay some five miles away. The horses leaned into the harness as they took a steep grade and the sweat on their sides turned a pasty red as they slowed and the dust settled on them. Barely moving at the pace a man could walk, the coach topped the rise. At once, the driver hauled on the reins and hit the brake.

"Whoah . . . whoah-up there," he called to the six-up team.

Two men, their faces covered by bandannas, weapons ready, blocked the trail with their horses. Caught unaware, the shotgun guard didn't even try to test his speed and skill with them. Four more men rose from the brush along side of the trail and closed in.

"Stand and deliver," a burly man, with bushy ebon eyebrows, one of the pair in the road, commanded. His bandanna followed the contours of what must be a bushy, black beard.

"Why are we stopping? What's going on?" the high-pitched, querulous voice of a short, fat, ladies foundations drummer demanded from inside.

"What the hell do you think it is?" the shotgun replied testily. "We're bein' robbed."

"Robbery," a young woman squeaked.

"Hand down the strong box. Easy now, we don't want no accidents," the other road agent commanded. He pushed his hat back slightly, revealing thinning sandy hair.

Looping the reins around the brake handle, the driver complied. The two outlaws on the left side of the coach took the iron bound chest and carried it off to a flat boulder that thrust up above the scrub growth. One applied a cold chisel and small sledge hammer to the lock.

After three stout blows, the case cracked, but the hasp held. With a muffled curse, the robber set his tools aside and took out his sixgun. He set the box at a careful angle and fired into the lock. That elicited squeals of fright from the three female passengers.

"Hey, listen there, we got some girlies aboard," one of his companions remarked.

"You boys get that loaded up," the bearded one ordered. "While they're at it, you folks in the coach step out, please."

"Now, see here," the pudgy drummer complained. "You've no cause to rob us."

"Money's money, friend, it all spends the same," a tall, thin, angular man with large hands and feet,

46

jovially informed him. "Get movin'."

Timidly, the passengers dismounted from the mudwagon coach. Despite his trepidation, the portly salesman assisted the ladies and took a belligerent step out ahead of them. His actions brought a chuckle from the hardcases facing them.

"Say, lookie there, them two is purty," a huge, round-headed bandit remarked.

A buxom matron in her early fifties took a step forward and brandished her folded parasol at William "Big" Randall. "Kindly keep your vulgar remarks and lustful eyes to yourself."

That brought a shout of laughter from the huge outlaw. He turned to his smaller companion, who had shot off the lock. "Hey, Jimmy, d'ya hear that? Lady," he addressed the indignant matron, "who you think you are?"

"I am Naomi Mattingly and these are my nieces. And I'll thank you to be more respectful to womenkind."

"You're welcome, Lady Mattingly," James West came back with a mock bow.

"Nieces, huh?" Big Randall grunted. "I've heard that one before. Where you turnin' those chippies out, Mattingly? You savin' 'em for the fancy-Dans in Santa Fe?"

Outraged, Naomi Mattingly advanced on the huge outlaw. "How dare you!" she exclaimed as she laid into him with her umbrella.

Big Randall chuckled good naturedly and snatched the offending object from her grasp. "Now that weren't nice. Even smarted some. Seems as how we just might have to sample the goods before we let y'all go on. Can't have no inferior merchandise foisted off on the boys at La Fonda."

"None of that," the tall, lean outlaw snapped,

47

edging his horse closer, his Winchester now marking a spot on Big Randall's chest. "We came to rob these folks, *nothing else,* y'hear?"

"Awh, Lute," Big appealed to Luther Waller. "I was only lookin' for a little fun."

"Find it with the *Tiwa* squaws you favor, Big." Lute Waller directed his attention to the passengers. "Folks, if you'll just empty your pockets and purses and deliver the contents to that big oaf in front of you, we'll be mighty appreciative. Be quick about it now, y'hear?"

Grumbling the five passengers, including a gaunt-cheeked, hard-eyed individual who said nothing, removed their valuables and handed them to Big Randall. When they finished, Lute Waller waved casually toward the mudwagon.

"You can get back aboard, now."

Bearded Tom Henry nodded to the driver. "You can move 'em on out now. I'd make right good time, were I you."

The driver complied with alacrity. Once the coach had rattled off in a cloud of red New Mexico dust, the bandits gathered around the strong box. The contents, though slim, gave each man a hundred dollar share, with Tom Henry taking his usual double portion. For some unaccountable reason, Lute Waller found himself laughing wildly.

Chapter 5

Long shadows, etched starkly black in the orange light of the westering sun, signaled the end of another day. Charity Rose had pointed out a small butte to old Tom Uzzel and the evangelist's caravan camped there for the night. Parked tongue-to-tongue in the shape of a "V", the steep wall of the mesa behind them, the wagons formed a secure compound. A low, smokeless fire crackled and more of the burro meat roasted over it. With the advent of quiet, if not serenity, Charity left the camp to answer the call of nature.

On her return walk, she abruptly found Orin Smith standing in her path. His oily smile and barn door teeth expressed rather well his intentions. When he reached out and touched her shoulder, Charity had no doubt. Frightening images of the Baudine gang, their rigid organs exposed and ready, flashed through her mind and she cringed.

"Say, now, no call to treat ol' Orin like that, Missy," the hypocritical parson rebuked her in a wheedling tone.

"If you please, *Mister* Smith," Charity began. Orin cut her off.

His other hand, turned palm out, traced the line of

her jaw. "No sense in pretending, Missy. You've got the hots for me, I can tell."

Only silence, and a piercing glare answered him. After a short while, Charity stepped aside and walked around him. She snapped her fingers for Butch, who followed with only a single backward look. At once relief flooded over her. Charity felt considerable pleasure over the mildness of her reaction: She held her ground and coldly stared him down. Likewise, the decorum of her response: She let Butch show Orin his teeth. Perhaps, she considered, she was finally getting a handle on her emotions. The incident, though, created a new problem.

She knew now the cause of Deborah's hostility. Any woman who had a husband with a terrible itch had cause for suspicion and anger. The smart thing would be to ride on and leave a bad situation behind. Yet, she felt certain that the protective cover afforded by the traveling evangelist show would be necessary in order for her to get close to Lute Waller without him suspecting anything. She would, she decided, have to stick around.

A tightly made, pine log building fronted on a side street in the business district of Nacogdoches, Texas. Behind it was a large warehouse, filled with barrels of assorted sizes. Light and changeable, a warm breeze brought into the tidy office the sweet aroma of femented and distilled sugar cane juice. Seated in a tilted-back swivel chair, in front of a roll-top desk, Dermott Wilkes studied his visitor with a slightly scornful twist to his full lips.

"The way I see it," Concho Bill Baudine explained, "we've either got to be paid more up front, or make up the difference how we can."

Dermott ran a thick-fingered, beringed hand through his short, curly black locks. A condescending nod replied to Bill's attempt at justifying their looting of those they had been sent to bully. Small, deep-set blue eyes angled up to the hands of a Regulator clock that ticked tirelessly on the wall. He sighed.

"I'm due at a lunch meeting with the mayor, Mister Baudine, so this must, understandably, be brief. I sympathize with your position. Were it possible to compensate you and your men at a better rate, and still show a profit from my, ah, whiskey trade, I assure you I would. On the other hand, frightening people into compliance, or forcing their abandonment of the land is one thing. Killing and robbing them is quite another. The end result could be that we wind up trying to explain it to the Texas Rangers."

Baudine stirred uncomfortably and cleared his throat. "I don't see any good coming out of that."

"Quite right. So then, how do you propose to eliminate the undesirable activity and still supplement your coffers?"

Concho Bill had to worry that one around a bit to make sense of it. When he did, he produced a relaxed smile and clapped his hands firmly on his thighs. "The boys are takin' care of that right now. From what you've said and the complaints the other day, I still figure you make a difference between what's done to people and what's done to an institution?"

"I do," Dermott assured him.

"Well, then, like I said. The boys are workin' on it."

Fifty miles northwest of Nacogdoches, the small community of Overton awakened in the cool, dewy

51

morning to another day of casual, friendly business. Many of the families in and around Overton had roots back beyond the founding of the town. Their ancestors had moved there from the Fredonia country at about the time the round-eye Texicans had their rebellion against Mexico.

They proved to be the smart ones. Following the rebellion against Mexico, Sam Houston, himself an adopted Cherokee, had left Texas to go to Washington. In his absence, Stephen Austin attempted to drive all the Indians from Texas. He nearly succeeded, except for the fierce Comanches and the clever Cherokee, many of whom had already "gone white." That had all been nearly forty years ago, and another war had come along since. One in which the round-eyes and the *Tsa la gi* alike had joined Hood and the cause of the Confederacy. Still, the long ago betrayal by Austin rankled.

Not that the round-eyes were discriminated against in Overton. They lived peacefully beside their Cherokee neighbors and frequently married into one family or another. They all had a vested interest in the Carroll family bank. Six strangers likewise showed considerable regard for the Fredonia State Bank on this bright spring morning.

"It is an easy bank to open, *non?*" Frenchy Descoines observed rhetorically. "I could do it with my eyes closed. *Alons,* we wait until the Monsieur Carroll comes down town and opens it for us, *mon amis?*"

"Too bad Lute ain't here with us," Westley Noonan remarked. "He always liked peelin' banks."

"He has his own important work to do, as do we," Frenchy responded. "Ah, I believe that is the gentleman we wait for now."

A barrel-chested man with a rolling gait walked

toward the bank entrance. He paused there, fished a key from his vest pocket and inserted it in the lock. A full turn to the right and he grasped the knob. He entered and a few minutes later two men, clerkish types, and a woman, followed. Frenchy nodded in satisfaction and four of the six outlaws crossed the street, angled toward the bank and paused at the door.

"It is time to make a little withdrawal, *mais non?*" the dapper outlaw declared as he opened the rich hued, polished walnut and glass door.

Inside, Frenchy and his three companions produced sixguns and announced their intention. The woman squeaked in fright and the clerks slowly raised their hands. Frenchy walked through the swinging gate in a low rail and stepped close to Galv'ladi Carroll.

"As you must be aware, this bank is being robbed," Frenchy informed him lightly. "You will please fill bags with the money from your vault. The gold and silver are preferred, but currency will do. Hurry, if you will."

Galv-ladi, whose name meant Prominent Man in Cherokee, narrowed his eyes, taking in every detail of the man who menaced him. "Should I know you from somewhere?"

"I don't believe so. It doesn't matter. All you need to know is the combination to the vault and that I won't hesitate to shoot you. It would not be a killing wound, only most painful."

Reluctantly, Galv-ladi Carroll complied. Inwardly he seethed and he made diligent effort to make sure he remembered every feature of this man and the other three. The day would come when they would be found and made to pay. Fortunately he had recently shipped a considerable amount of currency off to

53

buy bullion as a check against fluctuating prices. There weren't more than six or eight thousand in the bank.

Half-round wooden racks came from the top shelf of the vault. Banker Carroll emptied them into a canvas bank bag. He fingered some wrapped stacks of bills, then tossed them in too. He fought his anger and the urge to snatch up the .45 Colt lying beside the quarter and half-dollar racks. When he finished he turned around.

Frenchy Descoines had a sardonic smile on his full, sensual lips. He executed a mock bow, accepted the bag and walked to the railing. "You have been most cooperative. Perhaps we shall pay a call again some time."

"Don't bother," Carroll choked out.

"Gentlemen," Frenchy addressed his companions, "have you finished with the clerks."

"Yep," Westley Noonan responded crisply. "All neat and tidy."

"Good day to you all then," Frenchy said back into the bank when he reached the front door. "And, ah, *merci beaucoup*."

"By damnit, Emma," Galv-ladi declared irritably, "we've been robbed."

"You needn't swear, Galv'," Emma Whitefeather said demurely. "But I sure as hell wouldn't say we've had a good day."

Outside the Fredonia State Bank, Frenchy Descoines and his outlaw brothers swung into their saddles and rode swiftly, but decorously, out of Overton.

Another two days' journey would put them in Santa Fe, Charity Rose considered as Tom Uzzel and

Orin Smith maneuvered the wagons into their usual defensive position for the night camp. Five days on the road with the evangelists had not improved Charity's disposition. During the last two, she had noted signs of Orin Smith working himself around to another pass at her. It could happen, she concluded, at any time. With a good two hours to darkness, Charity decided to absent herself from camp and cut down on Orin's opportunities.

Besides, they could use a change in diet. The burro had gone rancid and they had fallen back on corned pork and a slab of smoked bacon. Poor Deborah, Charity thought as she set out toward the small spring that burbled from rocks a half a mile away. The year-around supply of water encouraged the growth of grass and trees and should attract game. Wild boar would be especially good, she allowed, when she spotted the cloven hoofprints of several javalina. She rounded an out-thrust buttress of the low mesa and entered the sheltered oasis.

Immediately the harsh warning grunts and snorts of a herd boar came from the tall grass ahead. Charity froze. She couldn't see the javilina, although it was evident it could see or smell her. Fortunately she had taken the precaution to have a round in the chamber and the hammer back on her Marlin Pacific rifle. The hefty firearm felt most welcome in her grasp as she studied the blind terrain for any sign, then took a cautious two steps forward.

At once the grass rippled a short distance to her left front. Then she saw another serpentine swaying to the right. Two of them. And good sized by the disturbances they made. The wily feral pigs had been known to frequently attack men afoot. They seemed to know no fear and those who had hunted them swore the javalinas would charge, singly or in groups,

55

a firing Gatling gun. A chill oozed along Charity's spine. It appeared to her that the hunter had become the hunted. At her side, Butch bristled and cut to the right stiff-legged.

Another series of grunts, followed by a shrill squeal, came from that direction. Then a blue of dark brown broke from the grass. Butch uttered a short hunting howl and launched himself at the charging javalina's throat.

Just in time, for the second bellicose boar raced from concealment and hurtled toward Charity. Without thinking it through, her Marlin came to her shoulder and she felt the slight jar of its recoil. Quickly she levered out the spent casing and inserted a fresh round.

Less than thirty feet away the attacking boar appeared to have hit an invisible wall. Forelegs locked and spraddled, it came to an abrupt stop. A dark hole, oozing red, was centered in its forehead. Methodically Charity took aim again and sent another 305 grain slug into the enraged creature's brain. It squealed sharply, quivered and fell on its side. Charity chambered a third round and called Butch off the second boar.

"*Amach,* Butch," she called, using the Gaelic language, in which she had trained him to respond. "*Tar anso,*" Charity added after she put a bullet in the javalina's head.

Butch had the boar on its side and he jumped back at the command, then trotted docilely to his master after she shot the creature. Swiftly Charity used her sheath knife to slit the throats of her kills. The shots had attracted attention from the camp, she discovered a moment later.

Orin Smith and, oddly enough, Deborah came running up to her. "What happened?" Orin inquired.

"Getting us some supper. Wild boar ought to be an improvement over mushy corned pork."

"Oh, they're *ugly*," Deborah declared. Then the thought of roasted game, other than wild burro, penetrated and she smiled warmly for the first time. "They'll taste good, though," she added.

Business-like, Charity went about the necessary details. "It would be better if we had a horse to drag them back to camp."

"Deborah, you go get one," Orin commanded.

"You know I'm afraid of snakes. You go," the young woman replied.

"Why don't you, ah, both go?" Charity suggested.

Half an hour later, the javalinas cleaned, spitted, and roasting over hot coals, Charity took time to wash off the blood in a tin basin. Her ablutions completed, she turned around, towel in hand, to find Orin Smith staring admiringly at her over the rim of a coffee cup.

"You're a remarkable hunter, Miss Charity. Why, any man would be proud to claim you as his own."

Here it came, Charity thought with a start, and right in front of his wife. The man was an ass at best, a low-life bastard most likely. She gritted her teeth and tried to ignore his approach.

"That ferocious expression of yours has to be a front, Miss Charity," Orin blundered on. "Underneath you're just a woman, like any other, who needs a lot of lovin'. An' I reckon I know where you could go to get all you'd ever want."

Beyond Orin's hulking shoulder, Charity saw Deborah go dead white, then flush a nearly black crimson. Hurt and rage warred on the young wife's face. Charity's patience dissolved with that and she gave free rein to her tongue.

"You arrogant, miserable, sorry excuse for a man,

57

how dare you even suggest such a thing? You're insulting me and your wife. How she can stomach you I'll never know. Just so you have the record straight, I wouldn't sleep with you if you were the last male creature on earth. I'd . . . I'd rather make love to a snake!"

Orin's face flushed and he forgot entirely where he was. "You're sort of lippy for a young girl all alone, aren't you? Maybe I oughtta haul down them britches and give you a good spanking. Then you might appreciate a real man sniffin' around you."

Butch had raised up at the round of angry voices and came trotting over from the far side of the fire. He bared his teeth now, eyes like gold coins, casting a glint of death. Charity saw him and spoke tightly. *"Fan,* Butch. Hold," she repeated in Gaelic. Then she finished with Orin. "You are a disgusting bastard, Orin Smith. Keep your distance the rest of the trip or I might let Butch chew on you a little. He's half-wolf, you know. Sometimes . . . sometimes when I call him out he doesn't come."

Able to produce only a tight little squawk, Orin turned on one heel and stalked off to his wagon. He did not show up for supper, though the javalina tasted divine and old Tom managed to lighten everyone's spirits with a lively tale about a gambler he ran out of town in Nevada after the card-sharp had interrupted a particularly colorful sermon. Through it all, Charity never forgot the evil look Orin Smith had given her.

Chapter 6

Dust devils danced between the tall buttes that surrounded the canyon trail from Santa Fe to Las Vegas, New Mexico Territory. Heat waves shimmered in the direct sunlight, though the high altitude made the breeze and shadows quite cool. After a two day stop-over in the territorial capital, the evangelist caravan moved on toward Las Vegas. They now had only a half-day journey ahead to reach the small, though notorious, community. Charity kept close to Matilda Uzzel and had no further exchanges with Orin or Deborah Smith. Deborah's continued hostility confused Charity.

After her outburst at Orin, Charity expected that Deborah would come to see her, if not as a friend, at least as no threat. To the contrary, if anything, her enmity increased. To Charity it seemed as though Deborah now vehemently disliked her because she found Orin beneath her contempt. It was as though Deborah hated Charity for *not* being attracted to the fractious girl's husband. No matter the cause, the entire situation had become too complex for Charity to fathom. She would be glad when they reached Las Vegas. Ahead, a weathered, hand-lettered sign stuck out of a cairn of rocks.

LAS VEGAS 11 Miles
Don't go there.

Charity read it aloud and had to laugh. "Apparently someone hasn't too high an opinion of the place," she said to Matilda.

"Sodom and Gomorrah," Matilda responded. "It's Satan goin' up an' down in the world. I see that as a sign from Heaven, which we should abide by."

"Nonsense, woman," old Tom Uzzel snapped to his wife. "It's another heathen town to tame and claim for the Lord. Duty calls."

"You old fool," Matilda grated back. "You never listened to the call until I drug you down the aisle by the ear and made you see the light. And you a man past fifty at the time."

"Gawd works in mysterious ways, His wonders to perform."

"Don't give me that, Tom Uzzel," Matilda chided good-naturedly. "I witness," she went on to Charity, "when he gets to feeling the spirit, he could convert a grizzly bear."

"Praise the Lord!" Tom Uzzel cried, slapping his hands together and startling his team.

"We'll be in Las Vegas before nightfall," Charity observed.

"And we'll set up for the revival tomorrow night at the biggest saloon in town," Tom enthused.

Lute Waller slammed down the whiskey bottle hard enough to start some of the contents from the open neck. "I'm gettin' tired of hanging around this rundown line shack. I got an itch like there was ants in my longjohns."

John Dorsey snickered. "I know that itch well enough. What you need is one of those soft, slippery pouches to scratch it for you."

"Now you're talkin'. A feller lopin' his mule just ain't no substitute for the real thing," Lute returned. "What say we ride into Las Vegas and get our itches scratched?"

"We can't," Tom Henry stated flatly. "We're too hot."

"Well, I ain't," Lute snapped. "I didn't go stealin' no horses in broad daylight and let some sissyfied Eastern dude see my bushy-haired face."

"No call for that, Luther," Tom whined. "You may be my first cousin's third cousin, an' eight years older'n me, but it don't give you no leave to be insultin'. We *had* to take 'em while we had the chance. Just dumb luck that la-ti-da Englishman came along when he did." Tom appealed.

"Oh, all right, Tom. I was only raggin' ya. Truth is, I'm horny as a three peckered billy goat and I aim to do something about it. You fellers can go or stay as pleases you."

"We'll stay, I reckon. Ah, bring us some more whiskey, Lute, hear?" Tom requested. "An' maybe some sugar, beans, flour and a fresh side of bacon."

"Who pays for all of this?" Lute asked suspiciously, eyes narrowed.

"*I* do, of course." Tom fished in his Levi Strauss trouser pocket and produced a ten dollar gold piece. "Buy a big hunk of fresh beef loin if that drunken Mezkin got around to butcherin' this week, will ya?"

The prospect of a thick, juicy steak made Lute's stomach rumble. "You bet I will. Can't pass up a good thing like that. Next best thing to some poon is some nice red meat. I'll saddle up an' be gone from here. See you boys come supper time tomorrow."

Charity and the traveling evangelists arrived in Las Vegas at four-thirty of that hot, dusty day. From a good three miles away, one marvelous vision had drawn them onward. Towering above the buildings of town, a solitary windmill had been a beacon of salvation. They located it in the precise center of the main plaza of Las Vegas. The communal water supply tended to the needs of homes and businesses, and made a unique item of decor. Other towns might have their white lattice-work bandstands, or forbidding cannon, but Las Vegas offered visitors and locals alike crystal clear, superbly cold water to slake the desert's thirst. A large trough stood at its base and the weary travelers led their animals there in pairs.

While the beasts drank, and the humans refreshed themselves from a bucket and ladle, old Tom set to scrutinizing every business edifice around the plaza. At last he settled on the plastered adobe facade of an establishment that advertised its custom in foot-high, bold, black letters.

CLOSE AND PATTERSON'S SALOON
FINE SPIRITS • WINE • BEER
CARDS • BILLIARDS • GAMES OF CHANCE
Open Around the Clock

Another, smaller sign advertised: *See the Lady in the Gilded Cage!*

"That's it!" old Tom declared spiritedly. "That's where we shall rescue the lost souls of Las Vegas. I'll go make the arrangements right now. Come along, Orin."

He started off, a bit stiff-legged after the many hours on a wagon bench, white hair flying, round-domed "preacher hat" cocked back to reveal his high, sun-browned forehead. Laggardly, Orin Smith trailed the flapping coat-tails. Charity Rose made her own examination of the busy central square. She considered it too good a coincidence that she might spot Lute Waller in the throng of people in less than an hour after getting to town. Her hunch proved a good one, when not a familiar face resolved out of the crowd.

"Once we get a place for the wagons, I'll take the stock to the livery," Charity offered. "I know Reverend Tom will be busy and it's really no bother."

"Thank you, Charity. You're so kind," Matilda Uzzel burbled.

Charity rented a hotel room, from which she could watch traffic on the square, after stabling the horses. It also allowed her to get away from Deborah's malign stare. She left instructions to double-grain Lucifer and put clean straw in his stall. Also to provide space for Butch overnight. That cost an extra twenty cents. She didn't begrudge the expense for her mount and dog; the hotel room went at the exorbitant rate of two dollars a night. And that without bath.

She could wash up in the windmill trough if worse came to worse, she'd almost decided, when the clerk snippily informed her that for an additional fifty cents she could have warm water brought to the communal bath at the end of the hall. They went big for group ownership in Las Vegas, Charity concluded.

"Oh, how jolly," she speared the pimple-faced young clerk with her icicle tone. "Pretend you needed it filled yesterday and have it *hot*, not warm, and ready by the time I get to my room."

"Y-ya-yes, ma'am," he responded to the fiery

gleam in her eyes.

Charity awakened early the next morning. For the long, boring surveillance portion of her quest, she selected a conservative modern frock with a miniature forget-me-not floral pattern in dark blue, with tiered outer skirts, lace at the hems, a tight waist and low bodice, all tastefully set off with ruffles of damask lace. Her rich auburn locks were concealed by a wide-brimmed hat of light blue, with a broad swatch of veil that hung down the sides. She also wore a matching long-sleeved jacket, cut deep enough to conceal the clever little leather pouch rig Jorge Santima had designed for her at the leather shop in Dos Cabezas. In it, she comfortably fitted one of her brace of bird's head grip .38 Colt Lightning revolvers. So accoutered, she felt ready to face the day.

Outside the hotel, Charity went directly to the livery to see to Lucifer. Thoughts of the big black brought a smile to her lips. When the Uzzels had learned the name of her horse they had been scandalized. Throughout the journey it had given even the outwardly friendly Matilda a jaundiced eye. Still amused by it, she entered the stable through the tall, wide doors that stood open to encourage fresh air.

Immediately she froze at sight of a man's profile in the small office to the right of the aisle. Lute Waller.

"A whole day's rate?" Waller complained. "I'll only be leavin' him here until noon. Tom an' the boys are waitin' on me. So what's wrong with half a day charge?"

"Rules is rules," the wizened hostler informed him. "Twenty cents a day, box stall and feed. Pay up or let him stand at a tie-rail."

Charity hurried back to Lucifer's compartment, her mind speedily working out a plan. Lute had never seen her done up like this. Probably, after nearly nine months, would never have the least chance of recognizing her. That fit in with her purpose ideally. She petted Butch and told him he'd have to stay there a bit longer. Then she patted up her hair, put on her most inviting smile and timed her arrival at front of the stable as Lute Waller stepped from the office.

"Oh, hello, there," she said sweetly. "I'm afraid I nearly ran you down."

Taken aback, his lust drained the previous night by an energetic brown-skinned *puta* in the Mexican section of town, Lute Waller examined the petite, smiling young woman who spoke to him. A wide, engaging grin spread on his face. He removed his hat in a sweeping gesture and made a slight bow.

"An accident from which I would probably never have recovered. I haven't the pleasure of your acquaintance, as yet. I'm Luther Waller."

"Megan, ah, O'Donnel," Charity invented on the spot, giving him her hand. "It's my pleasure, Mister Waller."

"Oh, call me Luther. I feel we have been old friends for a long while."

Charity produced a coy giggle. "Oh, certainly all of two minutes, Luther. And Megan will do, rather than the formalities."

"Have you broken your fast, Megan?" Lute inquired, still retaining her hand.

"No, I haven't. Could you suggest a good place?"

Lute took her arm and twined it about his own. "Right down this way. Cafe La Gloria it's called. They got Who-way-vohs Rancheros that are out of this world."

Seated in the spicy-aromaed Mexican cafe, Lute and Charity perused the menu, painted on the wall

65

by an unsteady hand. A waitress brought then red clay cups, glazed on the inside only, of thick, rich chocolate. Charity sipped of hers and smiled when the waitress produced a small pad and a pencil.

"I'll have me then Who-way-vohs Ranchers with the watery beans in a pot an' fried cactus," Lute ordered.

"Dos orden de Huevos Rancheros, con frijoles ojllitas y nopales fritas, por favor," Charity rattled off in crisp, precise Spanish.

"Say, Megan, I sure got to hand it to you," Lute said in awe. "You can sure handle that Mezkin talk right proper."

"Thank you, Luther. I learned it as a small child."

"Down Mexican way?"

"No, in Arizona Territory."

Luther blinked but made no comment. Big yellow teeth showed when he smiled. They drank from their chocolate and ordered more.

"Have you been in Las Vegas long, Megan?" Lute inquired.

"I arrived yesterday," Charity told him truthfully.

"Good place to be from," Lute observed. "Far away from as you can get." He produced a braying laugh at his own witticism.

They conversed lightly through breakfast, which Charity found to be delicious as promised, then she rose and made her excuses. "That was a wonderful meal, Luther. I've a feeling I'll take all my meals here. Thank you so much. Now I really must go. I have so many things to take care of. Will I see you again?"

"Not this trip, I don't imagine. If you're here long, I'll be back in town in a few days. You're a mighty lovely lady, Megan."

"Why, thank you, Luther," Charity cooed. " 'Bye now."

Still bemused by his remarkable meeting with the attractive young Megan, Lute walked to the livery an hour later, his arms filled with packages he would take back to the Henry gang. He expressed sincere surprise when he saw Charity standing in the frame formed by the large, open barn doors.

"Why, Megan, what are you doin' here? I never expected another good-bye."

"I came for you, Luther," Charity answered levelly. "And I'm afraid I haven't been entirely honest with you. I'm here to take you in for murder and other heinous crimes, for which you're wanted here and in Arizona Territory."

"Now wait a minute, Megan, that sounds like . . ."

"My name's not Megan. It's Charity. Charity Rose. You remember that, don't you Luther? Now set those packages down and come along peacefully."

"It's you!" Lute yelled, shaken by her revelation. Some seven of his friends, fellow members of Concho Bill's gang, had died because of her. She was deadly, that he knew. Yet he had no other choice. He let go of the packages and dipped for the butt-stock of his .45 Colt. The girl, the one they had all raped some two years ago, put her hand under her frilly little jacket. What for? Lute still wondered that as his Peacemaker cleared leather.

He was still wondering it when the Colt Lightning that had somehow appeared in her hand exploded twice, quite rapidly, and twin hammers pounded his chest. It didn't seem fair, Luther thought as his knees sagged. He'd saved those women on the stage from rape. Didn't it count for something? Didn't one deed balance the other? The big .45, gone suddenly heavy, slipped from his grip. Charity took another step

67

forward and centered the black hole in the muzzle of her .38 Lightning on Lute's forehead.

A momentary wash of orange flame turned into the blackness of eternity for Luther Waller as his head snapped back and he fell twitching in the dust.

Chapter 7

Pigeons, fluttering and cooing in alarm, had barely settled down on the livery barn when the law arrived. Shootings tended to attract badges, something Charity had known since the age of five when her father had become a deputy sheriff in Havupai, Arizona. In Las Vegas, Charity noticed as she stood over the corpse of Lute Waller, badges came on stylish broadcloth suits.

"My God, a woman," were the first words that came from under the mustache on Joe Carson's face. Then the requirements of his office asserted. "You'd better let me have that iron, Miss."

Charity reversed her hold and extended the Lightning butt first. She also gave the lawman a fleeting smile. "In my purse is a letter of authorization and a badge from Havupai County, Arizona Territory, Marshal."

That simple formula, heard often enough by any lawman, staggered Joe Carson. "You're a bounty hunter?"

"Duly sworn deputy sheriff. I've been after Waller and several others for the murder of Sheriff Frank Rose."

"May—may I have your name?"

"Charity Rose. Frank was my father."

Tight-lipped, Joe nodded. "You'd better come to the office with me, Miss Rose."

Charity found ample evidence of a caring woman in the efforts to banish the stark plainness of the adobe-walled marshal's office and jail. Waist high wood paneling, a carefully draped flag, framed pictures and even a small white ceramic vase of flowers offset the mud bricks and iron bars. Another man in a dark suit and flat-crowned black hat lounged behind the desk, a tin cup of coffee hooked on one thick finger. A gold chain made double arcs on his vest and he smiled warmly at her appearance, bending upward the corners of his pencil-line mustache.

"This is Miss Charity Rose," City Marshal Joe Carson said by way of introduction. "Miss Rose, Dave Mather."

Charity took in the cold gray eyes, long, straight black hair and square jaw. "Mysterious Dave Mather?" she inquired in a small voice.

"Ah, my fame has preceded me, I see," Dave answered lightly. An unaccustomed warmth filled his eyes and he kept his gaze fixed on Charity.

"You, ah, you're a friend of Wyatt Earp and his brothers, aren't you?" Charity questioned.

"We're more than passing acquaintances," Dave evaded. "What brings you to Las Vegas, Miss Rose?"

"She just shot and killed Lute Waller," Joe Carson informed him.

Dave's craggy brows raised a fraction of an inch. "I assume you had cause?"

"Damn, Dave, you're taking this rather mildly," Joe injected.

"What am I supposed to do? Wring my hands and go into a tizzy?"

Despite the seriousness of the situation, Charity

70

had to stifle a snicker. To cover her lapse, she got directly to the business at hand. "Havupai County has a thousand dollar reward on Waller. I need your verification that I apprehended him here in Las Vegas, Marshal. Also he's wanted in New Mexico. If not on separate flyers, you'll find him with the one of the Concho Bill Baudine gang."

"By God, you *are* a bounty hunter," Carson spluttered.

"I'm in it for revenge, Marshal. But that doesn't mean that any reward money I happen upon has to be donated to charity."

Dave Mather burst out in a hearty guffaw. "That's a good one. 'Donated to charity.' A good shot, a quick mind and pretty, too. Joe, you're going to have to invite Miss Charity to dinner. Rita would love to meet her and I'd be right proud to be her escort."

"Now, Dave . . ."

"Don't 'now, Dave,' me, Joe. What Miss Charity has done won't exactly earn her bouquets of roses from our beloved justice of the peace. We owe it to her to make her welcome."

" 'Let the low—er lights be bur—ning, send their beams a—cross the waves . . .' " The tight-packed crowd in Close and Patterson's Saloon sang loudly, if inevitably, off key. The Uzzel revival had so far been a complete success.

So much so that old Tom decided that after he had the sinners come forward to give themselves to the Lord, he'd let Orin preach his favorite Temperance sermon. Toward that end, when the singing ended, Tom Uzzel swung into his Call to the Light pitch.

"Show me a sinner who doesn't cry for the Light of Gawd's love! No heart is so black, none so empty that it can't be illuminated by the Saving Grace of our Lord! Oo-oh, you sinners! Look within you and see the mark of Satan's power. Cast it out, I say. In the last town we came to, a woman who wallowed in the sins of the flesh approached me and said, 'Reverend Uzzel, there's nothing you can do for me. I'm lost and enslaved by the Devil.' Why, good woman, I said, there's always hope. 'Not for me,' she replied. 'I'm a young woman, but I am a widow with two small children. To feed my babes, I sold my flesh. How could there ever be salvation for me?' Well, then, I told her how and had her get down on her knees with me . . ."

Reverend Uzzel went on with his powerful appeal, illustrating the story of Mary Magdalene and casting out other examples of the fallen who rose again. When he reached the dynamic conclusion, not a dry eye could be seen among the soiled doves and bargirls of Close and Patterson's, nor for that matter among the "good" women of Las Vegas.

"Come down, come down, oh, ye of tarnished spirit. Come to the arms of the Lord!" old Tom bellowed.

Led by Lazy Liz, a somewhat aging lady of the night, Nervous Jesse and thirteen of the town's painted ladies trooped to the improvised altar and knelt before Tom Uzzel. As a tribute to the fire and brimstone he had generously laid about earlier, three of Close and Patterson's professional gamblers joined the repentant girls. Rev. Tom laid his hands upon their heads, one at a time and called out the Devil in them. With much praying, sobbing and confessing, the mood in the saloon buoyed into a celebration of reconciliation.

"Demon Rum!" Orin Smith thundered after his introduction. "More men have died by the bottle than by the forty-five! Brothers, Sisters, our great nation faces a crisis far more deadly than all the guns at Shiloh, or Gettysburg." Orin went on to illustrate every evil aspect of liquor. He concluded at last by quoting from a popular stage play of some years past, *Ten Nights in a Barroom*, which was enjoyed a revival in the atmosphere of the Temperance League.

" 'At dawn of day I saw a man
Stand by a grog saloon:
His eyes were sunk, his lips were parched,
O that's the drunkard's doom.

His little son stood by his side,
And to his father said,
Father, mother lies sick at home
And sister cries for bread.

He rose and staggered to the bar
As oft he'd done before,
And to the landlord smilingly said,
Just fill me one glass more.

The cup was filled at his command,
He drank of the poisoned bowl,
He drank, while wife and children starved,
And ruined his own soul.' "

Only a few recalcitrant souls had not been moved by Orin's impassioned appeal. His theatrics had reduced nearly the entire assemblage to dark reflections upon themselves. Then, before Rev. Tom announced the hoedown to follow, a single, resonant baritone voice came from the back, reciting *The Toper's Soliloquy*, a popular answer to the temperance movement in California some two decades before.

" 'To drink or not to drink, that is the question: whether 'tis nobler to suffer the slings and arrows of outrageous thirst or take up arms against the Temperance League and by besotting frighten them? To get drunk—to sleep it off no more. To get drunk without a headache, and walk straight when drunk—'tis a consummation devoutly to be wished. To get drunk—to sleep in the street, to sleep! perchance to get *took up*—ay, there's the rub! And thus the Law doth make sober men of us all; and this, the ruddy hue of brandy, is sicklied o'er with the pale cast of water—to lose the name of DRINK!' "

With a wild and gleeful yell, the formerly solemn gathering took on the aspects of a riot. Disheartened at the way his recent converts reverted to type, old Tom Uzzel later observed, with a heavy sigh, "Well Mother, it's back to business as usual."

Rita Carson, a tall, angular woman with a sweet, heart-shaped face, long, straight black hair, shoe-button eyes and high cheekbones, proved a gracious and consummate hostess. Shortly after the shooting of Lute Waller, Charity Rose had parted company with Tom Uzzel and his evangelist family. Considering what she had been involved in, she and they thought it best. What interested Charity most was the cool, speculative look she got from Deborah, far different from the implacable hatred that had radiated from the young woman before.

Charity spent the remainder of the day alone, took in the revival out of curiosity and the next morning accepted an invitation from Joe Carson to attend an informal supper at his home that evening. About noon, Charity noted, the Uzzels clattered out of

74

town, headed eastward for Texas. She bathed and dressed in a new frock she had purchased that day and waited in the lobby of the hotel for Mysterious Dave Mather.

He arrived on time, stylishly done out in a dark suit and polished boots. They walked the short two and a half blocks to the Carson house, a small, squarish clapboard structure on a large lot with several outbuildings. Rita Carson greeted them both warmly and drew Charity into the parlor. The Carson children, the oldest a boy of about eleven, turned out to be clean, mannerly and bright, much to Charity's pleasure and relief. Rita brought Charity "tea," which turned out to be sherry in a crystal glass, while the men had whiskey. After a brief discussion of the events that had brought Charity into their lives, Dave Mather asked her a pointed question.

"Where are you bound from here?"

"I don't know, Dave. I suppose back to Doz Cabezas."

"You mentioned the Concho Bill Baudine gang," Dave returned. "The word around is that a lot of that bunch are in Texas."

"Oh?" Charity came back. "Where specifically?"

"I'm not certain, Charity. I'll ask around if you wish."

"I do, Dave."

"Enough of this grim talk," Rita declared, rising. "Let's eat."

Their meal turned out to be remarkable in itself. Rather than the usual fare of boiled this and gravyed that, the dishes were light and appealing. The men had just pushed back their plates, in contemplation of the promised pie to come later, when a knock sounded at the front door. Little Steve Carson answered it and came into the dining room a moment

75

later with one of Carson's deputies.

"Marshal, I thought you'd like to know. Tom Henry and his gang are in Close and Patterson's."

"Are they obeying the gun ordinance?" Joe inquired.

"I don't know. Ol' Dooley came dustin' over from the saloon to tell me."

"Ummm. I suppose there's nothing for it but to go and see for myself," Joe decided, sliding back his chair.

"Oh, Joe, do you have to go now?" Rita asked apprehensively.

"Look, darlin'," Joe explained, hands on his wife's shoulders. "Our high and mighty J.P., Henry Neil, might not give a rip what happens in this town, but I do. Besides, it's my job."

Rita bit her lip but said nothing. Joe departed with his deputy, while Dave lighted a cigar. Charity and Rita began to pile dishes on the drain board of the kitchen sink. The children had mercifully whisked from sight following the meal. After a few silent moments, Charity began to notice the loudness of a ticking clock.

"I wish he had stayed with cattle raising," Rita blurted out suddenly.

Charity laid a sympathetic hand on Rita's forearm. "I know how you feel. My father was a lawman for as long as I can remember."

"And he got himself killed for it, too," Rita snapped bitterly. Then she sniffed back the tears that threatened to fall and patted her hair. "But Joe's my man and I'll stand by him no matter what he does for a living."

Dave Mather called from the dining room. "Better cut a big piece of that pie for Joe. I reckon he'll work up another appetite walkin' up town and back."

His well-timed remark brought a short trill of laughter from Rita. "Land, how that man can eat! But he never puts on a bit of fat." She turned away to dip water from a large pot heating on the stove.

"Your children are delightful, Rita," Charity offered as a change of subject.

"Why, thank you, Charity. To hear Mrs. Lundquist, that's the schoolmarm, tell it, they're absolute demons. Funny how we can never completely know our children. They can be one way at home and entirely the opposite in the eyes of others. Steve's a good example. Around here, he's always doing the chores, working hard and talking about being a lawman like his father. Mrs. Lundquist says that outside of teasing the girls and whispering in class, his main interest is in music."

Charity smiled her appreciation. "A well-rounded individual, I'd say."

"Or looking to gain favor. Mrs. Lundquist considers herself a gifted pianist," Rita answered archly. The clock chimed the quarter hour and brought back the worry to her face. "I wonder what's keeping him?"

Chapter 8

Soapsuds to her elbows, Charity Rose gave a little start when the back door banged open and Joe Carson stood in the light from the kitchen. His face flushed, eyes blazing, he entered, thumbs hooked into his cartridge belt, and spoke toward the dining room.

"We've got us a problem, Dave. That damned Tom Henry and his boys laughed me out of the place. The whole bunch is there, spoilin' for trouble. Henry told me they'd not put their guns up until they'd done what they came for."

"What's that?" Dave asked, rising and entering the kitchen.

"They plan a little revenge for the killing of Tom's cousin, Lute Waller."

"Someone must have forgotten to tell them it was a woman who did for him," Dave observed.

"Don't think it would make any difference this time," Joe responded. "They may still be wet behind the ears, not a one over twenty-one, but they're hog-mean and achin' for a fight."

Dave Mather took his guns from a peg on the wall and began strapping them on. "How many are they?"

"All four of 'em. An' Hoo Doo Brown's buyin' 'em

rounds."

"You can bet he won't be there when the trouble starts," Dave observed.

"Yep. I gave 'em half an hour to comply with the law or face the consequences."

Dave looked at the big wooden-cased Regulator on the wall. "That'd make it ten minutes past. We'd better get moving."

"Ah, I don't intend to shove my nose in it," Charity began hesitantly from the sink. "But with four of them to face, isn't some sort of strategy in order?"

"Right you are, Miss Charity," Joe Carson allowed. "Figgered to work that out on the way."

"Why not now? That way you can go over it on the walk downtown and eliminate any flaws."

"Good idea," Dave concurred. "And the first thing is that you're not to get involved in any way."

"Amen to that," Joe added.

"Now just a minute. I'm perfectly able to care for myself."

"No doubt you are," the voice of the law said sternly. "But I, for one, don't even want you to be packin' a gun in this town, period."

Charity gave Joe a momentary amused look. "Then maybe I should take it out of my shoulder rig, Marshal?" she asked, opening her overwrap to reveal the butt of the Colt Lightning.

"What are we going to do with you, woman?" Joe asked in exasperation.

"Let me help you," Charity came back, iron in her voice. "First of all, no matter how good you two happen to be, two to one odds are lousy to go up against. How many entrances are there to Close and Patterson's?"

"One. Two, actually. There's a tiny little door

79

behind the storeroom that's unlocked during business hours. The loading dock's closed tight," Joe informed her.

"All right, then. Chances are the Henry gang won't know about the back. So that means they're waiting for you to come through the front. I noticed last night that they had a gas lamp system in there."

"That's right. A carbide tank in the cellar. Herb Close has sent for one of those dynamos and is fixin' to put in them new 'lectric bulbs. Don't see much future in that, though." Joe Carson wandered in an attempt to get Charity off the subject.

"Let's stick to the problem at hand, Marshal," Charity cautioned. "Your chances would be a lot better if someone got in there and shut off the lights."

"That someone bein' you," Dave Mather suggested.

"Why not?" Charity challenged. "If it's like the carbide systems we have in Dos Cabezas, there has to be a main line and a key valve to turn it off. A simple task for a, ah, saloon girl."

"Now, just a minute, Miss Charity," Joe burst in. "How can you get away with looking like a painted cat?"

"Among the clothing I brought along, I, ah, happen to have a dance hall costume. Part of my occupational equipment, you might say. If you stop all this silly wrangling, I'll have enough time to get to the hotel, put it on and be in place before you come through the door."

"That's too dangerous," Dave Mather charged.

"No it's not. And besides, I want to see that the hurdy girls are out of the line of fire."

"You'll not take that hog-leg of yours?" Joe asked suspiciously.

"No. I'll leave it behind," Charity assured him with a twinkle in her eyes, and the image of her small pocket pistol in her mind.

"You men can't be taking her seriously," Rita Carson protested.

"We weren't at first," Dave Mather assured her. "But we are now. What she says make sense. Only we've got to stop gabbing about it and start doing something. Time's short."

Not even Charity believed a woman could change clothes so fast. Decked out in her dance hall outfit, Charity entered Close and Patterson's saloon through the back door at five minutes to ten. With a practiced grace, she eased her way into the background activity and soon became anonymous, except for the avid, hungry looks from the customers of various ages. She managed to catch Lazy Liz's eye and motioned her to the bar.

"Listen close," Charity began without preamble. "We haven't got a lot of time."

Quickly she laid out what was in store. Liz agreed to warn the other girls and have them depart for upstairs rooms or a safe place away from the bar. With that part of her plan in action, Charity worked her way toward the Henry gang, who stood, ugly-faced, at the center of the mahogany.

"Look at that one's rear," Big Randall observed of her. "It moves like two tom-cats in a gunnysack."

"Hi, boys," Charity greeted. "In town for some fun?"

"We're here for some killin' needs done," Tom Henry snarled back.

Charity made a round "Oh" with full lips and tossed her auburn locks. "Surely you have time to enjoy a drink with li'l ol' me, beforehand, don't you?"

"You bet we do," John Dorsey eagerly agreed.

"Dorse, don't get to . . ."

"Awh, Tom," Dorsey interrupted. "We don't know he's even comin' back. 'Sides, the one we're lookin' for probably won't show tonight. Com'ere, pretty thing."

Cringing inside, Charity let the bandy-legged outlaw put his hands on her bare arms. He steered her to a place along the bar and called to French Pete, the bartender, for another round. Although Pete knew her not to be one of the regulars, he dutifully set a standard shot glass of strong tea in front of her and handed her a worn, smudged poker chip.

"Cheers, boys," Charity toasted, her glass lifted high.

With ritual repetitions of the salutation, the whiskey level went down swiftly. Charity located the thick, copper pipe at the far end of the bar that had to be the main line for the carbide lamp system. Smiling broadly, with a signal to French Pete for another round, she ran a finger along the jaw line of John Dorsey's face.

"Let's you and me go over there and talk," she suggested.

They sauntered to the end of the curved mahogany, in a position farthest from the batwing doors. There Charity roughly shoved down her revulsion and reached out to rub Dorsey's crotch. Then she began what she hoped would be a believable pitch for too high a price.

"What say we go upstairs to a room and relax?" she inquired.

"Uh, oh, uh, I'd like that. Only Tom'd get all heated up over it."

Charity gave him a throaty chuckle. "Happens that's what I had in mind for you . . . get you all heated up. Besides, who's he to be bossin' you around?"

"He-he's the boss. Tom Henry. We, ah, rob stage coaches and rustle cattle."

Charity made her eyes go wide. "My. An honest-to-goodness longrider, right here at my side. Well, Mister Longrider, I've got an urge for some long riding from this," Charity coaxed, her fingers tightening around John's rapidly extending manhood. "What say?"

"We-ell, I, ah,"

"Only cost you twenty dollars."

"Twenty dollars!" John Dorsey burst out. "Honey, I don't want to buy you, only rent you for a little while."

"I'm good. The best you'll ever have. I'm worth twenty dollars any day of the year," Charity spat, lips forming a mock pout.

"Not to me you ain't. I can get it for two dollars from any girl in here."

"Then—then you just go get it that way if you want," Charity fired back, letting her contempt run free now.

Red-faced and frustrated, John Dorsey turned his back on her and stomped away. French Pete, his short, wavy black hair parted precisely in the the middle, lush mustache waxed to needle points, came over to her. He leaned close and spoke quietly.

"The bosses, they don't like strange girls coming here, working the place. Especially when they charge too high a price. Where did you come from?"

Charity gave him a close examination. Unlike most men of his calling, French Pete had little bulk or stature. Short, slight of build, he had the rangy, long muscles of an acrobat more than a barroom brawler. He made her think of engravings she had seen of the French-Canadian *voyagers* of an earlier era. He had cool, vivid brown eyes, honest eyes Charity considered them. She decided to trust him.

"Pete, I'm new in town. I'm here working for Marshal Carson." Quickly she explained the plan. When she finished, Pete surreptitiously slipped her the key to the shut-off valve. The time, Charity noticed on the clock above the player piano, indicated 10:09.

At precisely 10:10, Joe Carson stepped through the batwings, a cocked Smith and Wesson American in his hand. He'd not even turned left toward the bar before a hail of lead came from the Henry gang. Bullets ripped and tore into his body. Cries of alarm came from several customers and the saloon girls shrieked from their positions of safety. Dave Mather stepped in over the corpse, his right-hand Colt blazing rapidly.

He emptied it into the crowded young gunhawks and executed a flawless border shift. The instant the second sixgun rested in his right fist, the lights went out. Muzzle flashes lanced the inky blackness. More screams, then a soulful groan from the direction of the bar. A rattle of boot heels came from the rear.

"He's there!" a voice cried.

Another exchange of fire followed, then the bang of a door sounded beyond the storeroom.

"Lights now!" Dave shouted.

Charity turned the key, then remembered to shut it off. Each individual light would have to be turned off and re-started. French Pete came up from the cover of his beloved mahogany bar and struck a match. Quickly he got two kerosene lamps glowing. Grabbing up one, Dave stalked toward the open

84

archway that led through the storage room to the small rear exit. Whichever of the gunmen had chosen that escape route, they were long gone now. The low, narrow door, its upper hinge ripped from the casement, hung forlornly by the lower.

Dave ignored it, squatting to take stock of a series of red splotches on the worn floorboards. Whoever had come this way had been wounded. Charity called out to him from the main saloon.

"Dave, you'd better come fast. This one's about to die."

Dave returned to find William Big Randall stretched out, face squinched up and eyes tight closed, blood pumping from three bullet holes. Mather reached his side as he gave a horrible rattle, deep in his throat, sighed softly and expired with a tiny thump of his bootheels.

"Damn, we lost that one," Dave cursed.

"Maybe this one, too," Charity announced from where she knelt beside another of the outlaws.

"Jim West," Dave identified the gunhawk. "That's a nasty hole."

"I'll send for Doc Ambrose," French Pete offered.

"Yeah, do that, Pete," Mysterious Dave agreed. "Tell him Joe's bad hurt."

"What about that one?" the startled barkeep inquired of West.

"To hell with him."

Charity looked around for something with which to block the hole in Jim West's chest, which blew a froth of large, pink bubbles. With a sucking chest wound, she knew, he'd soon drown in his own blood, or suffocate for lack of air. From the sawdust near an overturned table she retrieved a silver dollar and fitted it across the .45 hole. West's labored breathing eased a bit.

"Looks like all that's going to happen here," Dave observed. "I'll go to the jail for a stretcher. Will you be able to take care of yourself?"

Charity lifted James West's Remington revolver from the floor. "I think so. Hurry, Dave."

Doctor Clayton Ambrose entered Close and Patterson's only seconds after Dave departed. His quick examination told him that he could do nothing for Joe Carson. He came to where Charity sat in a chair overlooking the wounded outlaw.

"Hummm. Be damned. One of the Henry gang," Doc Ambrose observed. "Reckoned they'd get their come-uppance sooner or later. Joe get him?"

"Joe never had a chance. They shot him to doll rags the moment he came through the door," Charity answered.

"Dave Mather, then. He's one hell of a shot. I can plug these other two holes here, but I'll have to get this one some place clean to deal with that chest wound," Ambrose went on, becoming the professional again.

"He's going to jail, Doc," Mysterious Dave Mather rumbled from the doorway. He pushed through the batwings and started forward with the stretcher. "I'm not giving him a chance to get away. That son of a bitch is going to hang."

"He's seriously injured, Dave," Doc Ambrose protested. "I must take him to my place and operate."

"You'll do nothing of the kind," Dave declared in a hard tone. "If he dies in jail, well and good. If not, he swings."

"Now, Dave . . ."

"None of that, Doc. I'm the law here now. I want him behind bars. Tom Henry and John Dorsey got away. One of them's wounded, but I wouldn't put it past them to try to rescue West. So he stays locked up. End of conversation, Doc."

"Well, I won't be responsible . . ."

"That's right. I am."

Charity Rose accompanied Dave Mather to break the sad news to Rita Carson. The new widow listened with a hard face, which quickly dissolved into tears and anguish. She came into Charity's arms and sobbed wretchedly. Charity stroked her hair and made soothing sounds. And she found that she actually had tears for someone else's grief. The two younger Carson children didn't comprehend the significance of the late-night visit, but cried because their mother did. Steven, at eleven, went wild with his sorrow.

"I'll kill them!" he screamed, face scarlet, eyes streaming tears. "I'll kill all of them. You bastards . . . you sonsofbitches . . . *I'll kill you all!"*

Dave took the quaking, hysterical boy in his arms and spoke softly, while he smoothed the lad's sleep-rumpled hair. "Take it easy, Steve, it's an awful thing but we have to face it calmly. Cry, son, cry and get it out of your system. You have to be a big man now."

"Daddy, oh, Daddy!" Steven wailed.

Over the shaking shoulders of the boy, Mysterious Dave looked helplessly at Charity. She could only shake her head and make soothing sounds for Rita and the little girls. Through it all, the sorrowful night, and bleak day that followed, Charity began to perceive an aura of mutual affection developing between her and Dave.

Chapter 9

"I don't care if he rots and falls apart in there, Doctor," Dave Mather declared with such vehemence that the fat, blue-gray pigeons under the eaves of the marshal's office and jail gave startled coos and fluttered away. "I'm not letting him go somewhere so those hair-pin friends of his can break him out. West stays in the jail."

Three days had gone by since the shoot-out at Close and Patterson's, and Joe Carson's funeral completed only an hour ago. Although gray and waxen, his breath shallow and liquidy, his body gaunt and wasted by lack of nutrition and the ravages of his wounds, James West remained in the Las Vegas jail. During that time, Charity and Dave saw a great deal of each other. Although desolate, Rita Carson had stood up to the ordeal, her dark haired, blue-eyed brood solemn and quiet. Charity had moved into the Carson house, at Rita's request, leaving behind the hotel.

She suspected Mysterious Dave Mather to be behind this offer, in order to have her closer and easier to protect. The children loved Butch, naturally, and he reveled in the attention they lavished upon him. Rita became inured, if not philosophical, about her loss. She would stay, she declared. Already, Mister Purdy at the general mercantile had offered her a job clerking and doing his books. It paid more, even, than Joe had brought home. That, she acknowledged, because she didn't have to pay for ammunition or wages of temporary deputies out of her income. Despite Charity's disagreement with Dave over the treatment of the prisoner, their affection had grown more potent.

Last night, on the back porch of the Carson home, Dave had kissed her. She didn't need any artifice to kiss him back with equal fervor. Today there was a final meal to get through at the Carsons', with family and friends gathered. Then, Charity had readily agreed, the two of them would take some time away to enjoy each other's company. Even the latest argument with Doc Ambrose, which she overheard on her way to the jail office, wouldn't dampen her enthusiasm for that.

Dave was not a handsome fellow, short, though well-proportioned, polite and gentle-spoken. It gave him a ready appeal to women. He had the manners and ready flattery of a politician. Or of a bunko-steerer, Charity reminded herself as she opened the door to the marshal's office. Dave's happily beaming countenance assured her once more.

"Doc, you'll have to excuse me now. We're expected at the Widow Carson's," Dave apologized.

"So am I, if you recall," Doc Ambrose responded testily. "And I'll assure you I won't bring this up there."

"You'd better not. Rita would run you off with a broom," Dave said jokingly. "I see you're ready, Charity."

"I certainly am. I had to come all the way down here to fetch you, too. You men are terrible about time and dates."

"Aren't we though," Doc Ambrose agreed. He unconsciously preened himself in the presence of the lovely young lady, the soft, delicate fingers of his right hand brushing at his flowing white mustache.

"Come along then. I'll be the talk of the town with two handsome escorts."

The funeral supper went well, considering its purpose, and the guests departed before dark. Charity spent a restless night, sleeping on Steven's bed, while he used the sofa in the parlor. She awoke to bird-song and bands of pink and purple as the gold disc of the sun rose over the distant jumbled mountain ridge. Terrible groans came from the windmill in the plaza as it barely turned in a light, fitful breeze. It would be hotter than the devil's dooryard, Charity speculated.

Mysterious Dave Mather must have experienced the same evaluation of the weather. When Charity and the two Carson girls went to the general store for coffee, flour and sugar about ten in the morning, Dave hailed her on the street.

"Why don't we make our little jaunt for along toward evening?" he asked. "It should be pleasant by then. Perhaps a picnic supper out at Cottonwood Spring?"

Charity gave him a grateful smile. "I'll be ready at four. For a while this morning I thought we might go as planned and simply melt down into our shoes."

Dave grinned boyishly. "I had the same vision. Either that, or we would have to have gone skinny-dipping to keep from drying up like mummies."

Charity gave the Carson girls a suggestive shove. "Go on in and get a licorice stick each from Mister Purdy, girls."

They hurried off with squeals of delight. Charity leaned close to Dave's ear. "We might have to take that swim, no matter."

Dave called for her a little after four. He had a sprightly shay, with white fringe and a checkerboard top of black and white squares. A huge hamper sat behind the padded spring seat, from which the long neck of a green, corked bottle peeped out at one end. Charity had brought her own hamper, a thick quilt, and a table cloth. She set them in beside the other and let Dave hand her up on the seat.

"Hang on. We want to put this town and all its woes far behind us," Dave announced with a laugh.

With a brisk slap of the reins on the horse's rump, the shay started off at a good clip. Charity had to hold onto her hat, despite the windless day. Laughing together over nothing, they trotted out of town.

Moss and lichens covered the stone basin that formed Cottonwood Spring. Even the shadows, under the leaves of the broad, squat trees seemed to be green. Dave took the heavy lead ground anchor from the shay and secured the horses. Then he began laying out the items from the back.

"What all did you bring?" he inquired.

"Oh, the usual," Charity replied. "Fried chicken, pea salad, some cornbread. What's in that hamper of yours, besides a bottle of wine?"

Dave pulled a long face. " 'The usual,' " he mimicked her. "Fried chicken. But I also brought some cold roast beef, and the chicken is really squab, six of them. We're going to have to burn a lot of energy to consume all this."

"I'm not in the mood for a long walk in the desert, if that's what you have in mind."

Dave moved closer, slipped an arm around Charity's shoulders. "I've never been much for walking. I, ah, had some other things under consideration."

Charity turned in toward him, their lips only

91

inches away. "Such as?"

Their kiss lasted an eternity. Charity felt comfortable and safe in Dave's strong arms. He held her tightly and pressed himself to her. The long, solid presence of his aroused manhood, warm against her lower belly, thrilled, rather than revolted her. Despite her frequent feelings to the contrary, Charity found herself excited.

Her arms circled his neck and delicate fingers toyed with his hair. Charity murmured deep in her throat and their lips parted.

Her eyes had gone soft and starry and a winsome smile curved up the corners of her mouth. Dave kissed the tip of her nose. Charity ran one small hand down Dave's chest to his waistband.

"You said something about swimming?" she asked, a part of her mind highly amused that the world, or at least her love-life part of it, had come full circle.

"It's a nice way to work up an appetite. Only . . . I can't swim."

"Then dog-paddle," Charity instructed him as she began to unbutton her blouse.

There was nothing mysterious about Dave Mather with his clothes off. He was amply and totally male. Often, since he'd first seen her lovely face and delicate hands, Dave had tried to imagine Charity in the nude. The reality stunned him.

Her hard, lean body, well muscled from her self-imposed regimen of physical training, was supple and faintly colored by frequent exposure to the sun. Small, pert breasts stood impudently upright, the nipples swelling under his gaze. A shiver of delight coursed through Dave's frame as his eyes followed the arrow lines downward to her pelvis.

Suddenly awkward as a callow youth, Dave took a

hesitant, half-step toward her. Charity rapidly closed the distance and they embraced.

Electric shocks surged through them both at the delectable contact of bare flesh. Charity's tongue wove a pattern of fire and ice in Dave's mouth. Before long they both quaked with the demands of their building desire. Charity felt herself let go and become all wet and ready. Forcefully she broke away and jumped feet-first into the cool water of the spring.

"C'mon!" she cried gleefully.

Confused, Dave followed her. She splashed him and swam a few strokes away. Dave hurried after, aware his actions were much like those of a stallion after a mare in season. He caught Charity from behind and hugged her close to him, his rigid, tingling organ pressed into the cleft of her buttocks. Charity shivered and squirmed around in his grasp.

"Ummm. That's much better," she said softly.

Her warm, firm hand adjusted his position and, to Dave's surprise, inserted him easily. "Oh, Dave," she spoke again, quiet and closer to his ear. "I didn't plan for this to happen, but it's . . . it's so *wonderful*."

They began a slow, satisfying rhythm, rocking in the soothing water, blissful and abandoned of all cares. When the universe exploded in a mutual welter of release, Charity further amazed Dave with her joyful declaration.

"Oh, Dave, thank you, thank you for a happy, happy day. Now, let's eat, I'm ravenous."

Yellow lamplight filled the parlor of the Carson house. Rita sat in a wing-back chair by a small table, mending a pair of Steven's trousers. Charity sat to her left, on the opposite side of the table. After the final stitch, and a quick, solid bite with small, even

93

white teeth, to sever the thread, Rita looked up and spoke in her gentle, mother-to-child tone.

"You know, Charity, we've spent a lot of time talking about Joe and me, and the kids. But I know very little about you. I feel that I've slighted you, because of my upset."

"Not at all, Rita. Actually, there's very little to tell."

Rita set Steve's trousers aside and reached for one of Josephine's small frocks. "Oh, come on, now. I know, of course, that you are a bounty hunter. Though why a woman would ever want to do that escapes me. But you weren't born one. How did you learn what to do, how to go about it?"

Charity smiled sadly and rose from the chair. "Can I get you more coffee, Rita? I'm going to freshen mine and then I'll reveal all, as they say."

"No, thanks. I've had enough." Rita gave up a tiny, girlish giggle. "Hurry, though, I'm dying to know your deep, dark secrets."

When Charity returned, she made herself comfortable and then launched into a recitation of her past. "I grew up as a substitute for the son my father never had. Oh, I didn't resent it; to the contrary I loved it. I learned so much from him. By the time I was eight, he was sheriff of Havupai County. I hung around the office and cleaned the jail. There weren't many books in Dos Cabezas then, so I got extra reading practice from wanted posters.

"I learned all the terms to describe a person and I used to visualize the wanted men in my mind. That also gave me a rather broad education in the villainy man is capable of. While other kids my age were still struggling with Dick and Sue in their McGuffey readers, I wrestled such terms as mayhem, public disorder, mopery, and murder. My father taught me to read law books, too. And to fish, swim, and hunt. Then, when I was thirteen, something happened."

"A boy?" Rita asked in a quiet voice.

Charity nodded, then went on. "All at once I wanted to wear dresses instead of pants, bows in my hair and pretty dancing shoes. Frank's tomboy, as they used to call me, died along with my innocence."

"And the bounty hunting?" Rita prompted.

"You knew my father had been killed by escaping prisoners," Charity's voice grew husky as she described her father's murder and her degradation by the Baudine gang. She related her efforts so far at tracking them down and the results. Wide-eyed, Rita listened with rapt attention. Charity's narrative reached Las Vegas and the Lute Waller affair and she concluded with a surety she would have not expressed before.

"I'll not stop now. Not until the last one of Baudine's men answers for what they did."

"Good for you," Rita responded with considerable heat. "I envy you, Charity, 'cause I'd sure like to take care of those murdering scum who did in my Joe."

The vehemence in Rita's voice sent a chill down Charity's spine. She'd certainly not want the young widow mad at her, she concluded.

A bell jangled in the city marshal's office even before Mysterious Dave Mather entered the building. He yanked the offending, conical-shaped instrument off its hook and shouted into the small grille.

"Marshal's office, Las Vegas. What is it?"

He quickly put it to his ear in order to hear the tinny voice at the far end. "Dave? Is that Dave Mather?"

"Who else at this gawd-awful hour?" Dave demanded when he saw the hands of the Regulator

95

sitting on 6:30. "Hell, the birds ain't even awake."

"U. S. Marshal's office, Santa Fe, here. You had a warrant on Tom Henry and John Dorsey?"

"Sure did," Dave answered in a clipped manner. The newfangled telephone of Alex Bell's still intimidated him some.

"They were captured over at Mora, New Mexico, yesterday. One of our deputies is enroute to Las Vegas now, with them in custody."

"Well, thank you very much."

"You're welcome. Good-bye. And don't forget to ring off, y'hear?"

Shit! Why a person would want to keep a bell in their house, that anyone in the world could ring at any time of the day or night, he could never understand. At least, Dave relented, it brought the news Rita would want to hear faster than a rider or the mail. It would wait, though, until the ladies had a decent chance to wake up. Dave still felt terrible about Joe's death. Somehow he believed himself to be responsible. *He* should have gone through the door first. Such an impression made him even more solicitous toward the poor young widow with three small children. And he'd been drinking too much. Far more than his usual wont.

Charity was good for him in that respect. He curbed his desire for whiskey when he knew he'd be in her presence. With her, he'd get through this. Well, he planned silently, first stop for breakfast, then go tell Rita that the rest of the Henry gang had been rounded up.

96

Chapter 10

Dogs yapped and a flock of barefoot, yelling boys accompanied the U. S. Marshal and his prisoners down the main street of Las Vegas. Late in the afternoon of the Friday following the announcement of their capture, Dave Mather waited on the shaded stoop of the marshal's office to take them off the deputy's hands. Rita had been delighted and the only dark spot for Dave had been Charity's remark.

"At least now, with them all accounted for, you can have that poor boy treated for his wound. It's a wonder he's lived so long."

They'd made up for that later, in the sweet, fragrant hay of the Carson stable. Charity had been wild and uninhibited in her love-making. The powerful engine of her healthy, young body had drained and exhausted Dave, while their mutual attention to giving more than they received transported them both to new heights of rapture. Dave still hummed and tingled from it as he waited for the prisoners.

"They came along nice and quiet," the deputy marshal informed Dave after the formalities.

" 'Course, Tom Henry's got a hole in his leg. That might account for some of it. Ol' Tom claims they were ambushed, that they shot in self defense and there's no call for them to be arrested."

Dave produced a rueful smile. "If you call shootin' down a man when he walked through the door of a saloon being ambushed, then that's what Joe Carson did to them. He ambushed them so bad he died of it." He looked at the prisoners, newly installed in the same cell with Jim West. "You ought to be glad you don't already have ropes around your necks, instead of being safe in that cell."

After the deputy departed for the hotel and some well-deserved sleep, Dave got to thinking about what he had said. He knew lots of people around Las Vegas who would be happy not to wait for a trial before hanging the Henry gang. They'd bullied and buffaloed nearly everyone at one time or another. Who'd miss 'em if they got strung up? Such thoughts gave a man a powerful thirst, Dave concluded as he got up and headed for Close and Patterson's.

"—ing is, they've got no kin, never done a lick of honest work and ain't worth the expense of a trial," Dave Mather lectured an attentive audience in Close and Patterson's.

French Pete kept the bottles coming, toting up Dave's tab. Four hours and a lot of whiskey had gone by since Dave came there from the marshal's office, about sunset. He had done a lot of speculating on the fate of the Henry gang and the beneficial effect their demise would have on the community. None disagreed with him. In fact, over the past ten minutes, several erstwhile pillars of the community offered encouragement toward the idea of a necktie party.

"They're guilty as hell," Dave thundered suddenly.

"I was here and saw it. Cut down poor Joe without a how-dee-do. They'd have ventilated a few more folks if the lights hadn't gone out."

"So what are we waitin' around here for?" a cowboy from the X-Bar-X demanded.

"Yeah!" a chorus answered him.

"Go over to Purdy's and get some rope," Millard Cramer suggested.

Dave Mather blinked owlishly and downed the last of the whiskey in his glass. Then he stood, gravely, and quite without precedent, led a delivery on his own jail. A yelling, laughing crowd followed him. They picked up a few stray youngsters, Mexican and Anglo boys, who cavorted in their wake, imitating the actions of the adults. At the jail, the sound of their approach struck terror into the Henry gang.

"Oh, my God, they're comin' for us," John Dorsey moaned.

"Dave Mather's a sound lawman," Tom Henry opined. "He won't let them have us."

When the door banged open and the mob, led by Dave Mather, entered, Tom Henry nearly lost his evening meal of potato soup and fried fat back. He and Dorsey shrank back into a corner and Jim West wailed in horror.

"You can't do this. Please, don't!" John Dorsey begged in a hysterical screech.

"Get a flat-bed wagon out in the plaza," someone shouted toward the rear of the lynch mob.

Dave Mather unlocked the cell and men poured in. Quickly they grabbed Henry and Dorsey and roughly dragged them outside. West they carried on a litter in order to keep his blood from dripping and smearing the vigilantes. This required little effort as fever and malnutrition had wasted his once robust frame to a mere shadow. The mob stormed down the street and surged into the plaza. The eager avengers had not been able to locate a wagon, so the mob hustled their victims to the platform across the lower level of the mill. One rope already dangled from high above.

"Please, save me. Please, please, someone help me," Jim West begged. "Oh, have mercy on me!"

Despite their reputations as killers and thieves the three doomed and trembling men were all less than twenty-one years old. Youth and ignorance were no excuse to the vengeance-hungry mob. One of them grabbed Henry by the hair and forced him to look at the rope.

"Ain't you scared, Henry?" the man demanded.

Tom took a long look at the hastily-formed noose, choked momentarily, then finally muttered, "It's pretty tough to be hung, but I guess I can stand the consequences."

By no particular design, West was the first. The rope jerked him off his litter and swung him high into the air. In their blood frenzy, the mob failed to tie the wounded man's hands. He grabbed frantically onto the rope at his neck. Pulling himself up, he began to scream incoherently.

"Mother! Oh, Mother, help me!"

Then his ill-fitting trousers dropped low on his waist and threatened to continue to his boot-tops. "Please," he cried, "button my pants."

Charity Rose had heard the roar of the mob when they left Close and Patterson's, and correctly identified its meaning. She stepped from the front porch of the Carson house and found Rita Carson in the parlor.

"I think a mob is going after the prisoners," Charity informed the widow. "Which, I suppose, means Jim West's suffering will soon be over."

"Enough! Enough to pay for Joe?" Rita asked bitterly. "Charity, would you fix the children some chocolate? I'm—I'm feeling a little lightheaded."

"I'll be glad to." .

Charity busied herself with the task for several minutes, then called a question to Rita. When she received no answer, she went in search of her. Rita was nowhere to be found. Another glance around the parlor drew Charity's attention to the mantel over the fireplace. The Winchester that usually hung there was gone. Quickly Charity rushed from the house, headed for the roaring crowd in the plaza.

Kicking and squawling, Henry and Dorsey were made ready to go up next. A lance of yellow-orange flame came from the darkness at the edge of the plaza and a gunshot reverberated off the building fronts. Rapidly, three more shots sounded. Henry and Dorsey fell to the platform, still much alive, although terribly wounded. Tom Henry, tears streaming along with the blood, crawled to the edge of the platform and worked his mouth desperately.

"Please, please, someone shoot me through the head. I'm hurt awful bad and am like unto die."

An accommodating vigilante obliged him. "Looks like the widow wants them boys shot," he observed in a commanding voice.

Then everyone took it up. Within seconds John Dorsey, Tom Henry and the dangling body of James West got filled with holes. A sudden, awed silence descended on the plaza, broken only by the creak of the hanging rope over a wooden beam.

Charity Rose reached Rita Carson at that moment and wrestled the Winchester from her hands. The

101

blank, frozen expression washed from Rita's face and she slumped against Charity's shoulder. Great, wracking sobs came from deep within her breast.

"It's over, Rita," Charity soothed. "It's all done and gone."

"Yes, dammit! Couldn't they understand? I wanted them *all* to suffer!" Rita replied through heaving breath. "It's *really* over now."

Charity suppressed a shudder.

"This coroner's inquest was called today to look into the sudden, and violent, deaths of Thomas Henry, John Dorsey and James West. It is my decision as coroner that the aforesaid men, Henry, Dorsey, and West," the coroner dryly observed the next day, "met their just fate from the hands of parties unknown. So let the record show. And may God have mercy on their souls."

"Now what?" Dave Mather asked Charity over coffee at the Bon-Ton cafe.

"All this violence and tragedy has dragged me down more than I've let on, Dave. I, ah, think I'm going to show my heels to Las Vegas."

"Headed where?"

"You mentioned that Bill Baudine's gang was taking part in something in Texas, Dave. Have you learned anything more about that?"

"Yes, I have," Dave assured her. Before he could answer further, the deputy marshal who had brought in the Henry gang entered the cafe. Dave waved him over. "Here's the man who told me about it."

He introduced the marshal and Charity and asked for a rundown on Baudine's suspected activities. The marshal, eager for human company and a naturally gregarious individual, gladly complied.

"Baudine's supposed to have hired out some or most of his riders to that Carroll-Wilkes feud. On the Wilkes side, naturally. Federal revenue officers are sittin' that one out, ready to scoop up the survivors. It's a whiskey war, Miss," he went on to explain.

"The fightin's going on over around Longview, in the eastern part of the state. Chances are that's where they'd be found. What's your interest, if I may ask?"

"I'm hunting them down," Charity replied in a cold tone.

"This is the young lady I told you about," Dave explained.

That elicited a low whistle from the deputy marshal. "I rec'lect what you told me, Dave, but I swear she's too pretty to be a bounty hunter."

"Why, thank you, Marshal," Charity replied, batting her eyes. "Compliments are at a premium around this town."

Dave scowled at her. "Truth is, she gets complimented entirely too much," he said in jest.

"I'm interested in this feud, Marshal. It seems Concho Bill gets mixed up in such goings on quite often. There was the Johnstown War last year and now this."

"Not to mention that some of his boys ran with Tunstill's enemies down in Lincoln County," the lawman added. "I don't know much, except what comes in on government flyers. Seems like the sort of thing Baudine'd get hooked up with, though. If you're goin' after them, I wish you a lot of luck, Miss." The marshal rose, excused himself and walked to the counter.

"I can't talk you out of leaving?" Dave asked earnestly.

"No, Dave, you can't."

Early dawn found Charity Rose and Lucifer on the way to Texas. Butch sat in his usual place atop the packsaddle on Charity's pack horse. She covered close to five miles when Mysterious Dave Mather caught up.

"Charity, I really don't want you to go." Dave had started drinking early, or not stopped from the night before, Charity noticed.

"I have to, Dave. I'm going to ride over to Amarillo and take the train to Longview. One way or another I'm going to end this with Concho Bill."

"What about us? We're good together, Charity. I don't want to see that end."

"Who says it has to end? Longview should provide enough bounties for both of us."

Miffed by her assumption of control in their relationship, and obvious willingness to drop him to pursue her own ends, Dave rode along in silence, taking an occasional nip from a bottle he stored in his saddlebag. Charity frowned her disapproval yet said nothing. About an hour later they passed between two tall stone cairns, which supported a dilapidated, weathered sign.

"We're on Jinglebob land now," Dave observed. "Everything from here to the Palo Duro belongs to Jesse Chisum."

"That's a lot for one man to possess," Charity observed.

"Jesse Chisum's a *lot* of man," Dave informed her. "You could say he's the biggest thing around these parts. Short of Charlie Goodnight, that is. Ol' Charlie owns the Red River country. I mean, all of it. From Palo Duro Canyon on. The whole thing. Now, *that's* big."

Half an hour later they came upon a middling

large trail herd, the cattle freshly marked with Jesse Chisum's 4-X (XXXX) road brand. Dave hailed the trail boss cordially.

"You're ridin' Jinglebob range," the head drover said in a clipped manner.

"Yep. We know that. I'm Dave Mather and this is Charity Rose."

"I'm Phill, Dave. You're, ah, the lawman from Las Vegas?" inquired the drover boss.

"Former lawman. I quit this morning. We're ridin' over Texas way."

"Drop by the main ranch. Mister Chisum would be delighted to guest you for a night."

"Thank you, we'll try to do that," Charity injected. "We're headed for Longview."

The foreman scratched at the stubble on his chin. "Longview's a mite too close to Nacogdoches for the liking right now," he observed.

"Why's that, Phill?"

"There's a feud dusted up over there. Not to my likin' at all."

"Isn't the law doing anything about it?" Charity asked.

"Little 'er nothin'," Phill replied. "Frazer McCall is sheriffin' at Nacogdoches. Rumor has it he's in Dermott Wilkes' hip pocket. An' there ain't no law that'll side with those Longview Cha-roggies."

"Frazer McCall's in Nacogdoches?" Dave said faintly.

"Sure is, Mister Mather."

"Well, well, well. Ah, thank you for your information and hospitality, Phill," Dave said hastily. "We'd better let you get to your cows. G'day to you."

"And to you," Phill called over his shoulder as he loped after the herd.

A mesquite fire crackled in a ring of stones on the west bank of the Canadian River. Another day had passed since Charity and Dave had met the trail boss and the 4-X cattle. Dave had grown quiet and morose, drinking heavier all the while. Now, with supper over, he roused himself and turned reddened eyes on Charity.

"I think it's a better idea if you come with me to Dodge City," he announced without preamble.

"What do you mean, Dave? I can't do that. I'm going after Concho Bill."

"Nope. Dodge's the place for us right now."

"Please don't start on me, Dave. You seemed willing enough to go to Texas, why this Dodge City thing?"

"Uh, well, I hadn't wanted to say anything, but it's been on my mind a while now. You see, if we go to Longview, we're likely to wind up in Nacogdoches before it's all over. And Frazer McCall is there."

"What's that got to do with it?" Charity demanded.

"Well, a few years back, Wyatt Earp and I ran this dodge on some folks in Colorado. We made up some 'gold bricks' outta lead and gold plating. The, uh, upshot is, we sold one to Frazer McCall. When he found out he'd been took, he ran Wyatt and me out of town. Swore he'd get us on a bunko-steering charge if he ever saw us again. So, I can't go into Nacogdoches."

"All the same, Dave, I'm not going to Dodge City," Charity maintained, unconvinced as to the danger to Dave.

Dave started an angry reply, then cut it off and turned to his bottle. He continued drinking and sulking while Charity cleaned up after their meal.

She started making signs of going to bed when he roused himself and grabbed her tightly by the left biceps.

"By dang it, there ain't no other way to it. You *will* go to Dodge with me." Dave started to shake her roughly when Butch and a Colt Lightning interfered.

"Let me go, Dave," Charity said quietly as she started her squeeze on the double-action trigger.

Butch, stiff-legged, had all but closed his teeth on Dave's right calf. Through a curtain of whiskey fumes that fogged his brain, Dave make a quick estimate of his situation. Slowly his fingers relaxed.

"I'm sorry it ended like this, Dave. I truly am. Right now I'm not certain I would be safe around you for much longer. So, I'm going to keep this Lightning trained on you while you break my camp gear and load it. Lucifer's a good night horse and we shouldn't have any trouble. Saddle him up and load my other equipment on the pack horse. Then we'll say good-bye."

"Charity!" Dave cried in a strangled voice.

"Don't make it any more difficult, Dave, please. And, ah, we'll take your horse along a mile or so to make sure you don't get any bad ideas."

Grudgingly, Dave complied. While he worked he cast quick, nervous glances at the muzzle of the Colt Lightning. The slender .38 Long Colt muzzle never wavered from his shoulder blades. At the last, he decided to leave Charity's cinch loose. She'd fall ungracefully to the ground, he'd pick her up and they would laugh about it, kiss and make up.

Charity spotted it at once. "Tighten that properly, Dave. I don't want to have to shoot you."

"Hey, Char, it was a joke. I thought if you lost a little of your dignity we might be able to work it out."

"That we can't do, Dave. You were good. And I'll probably miss you, but I think I can learn to live with that. Good-bye, now."

Swiftly she rode off, not so much for fear Dave Mather would harm her as to keep him from seeing the tears that shone in her eyes.

Chapter 11

"Lute Waller has been gunned down?" the strangled shout from Concho Bill Baudine came out more a statement than a question. "Who did it? Who managed to get the best of him?"

"Take it easy, Bill," the unwilling messenger urged.

Baudine paced the large room of the two-story, plaster-chinked log house he and the gang occupied on a Wilkes farm in the hills north of Nacogdoches. He wanted to break something, smash and tear whatever he could get in hand.

"Uh . . ." the messenger continued uneasily. "It was a bounty hunter. Called him out in Las Vegas, at the livery."

"That's in the letter, for all the good it does. Goddamnit, there goes our connection on that end. We don't have a market for stolen beef any more, thanks to this. Who was this bounty hunter?"

"A-a-ah, a woman."

"Charity Rose!" Baudine screamed. "Damn that girl. How did she find him? She must have back-shot him, eh? Eh?"

"I don't know how she learned he was there," the young outlaw stammered. "Only that she called for him to surrender and he went for his gun. Now

Luther's dead."

"If we could pull out of here right now, I'd go after that bitch and finish her right proper. But damnit, we're tied down. I'd give anything to see her face again. Her and that goddamned dog."

"From what that letter I gave you said happened to Luther, I ain't sure *I* would," the messenger opined softly.

Outfitted in a stylish and fashionable new ensemble, Charity Rose stepped demurely from the railroad coach onto the platform of the station in Longview. She did so amid the admiring and appreciative glances of every male over the age of eight in the vicinity. A slightly built boy in his early teens, with shaggy blond hair, high cheekbones and gray-ringed blue eyes approached to take her luggage. Smiling sweetly, which caused a flush of pink to his tanned cheeks, she surrendered to him the satchel carpet bag and a trunk the porter set off.

"In the stockcar I have a horse and a large dog, though I think it best if I accompany you when you go for them."

"Yes, ma'am. Where to?" He indicated her bags with a nod.

"I'm new here," Charity said by way of explanation. "What's the best hotel in town?"

"The Stilwells run the Republic House, it's about the best anywhere," the gap-toothed lad responded.

Oh, my, a gap in his teeth, freckles, and yellow hair, Charity thought recklessly. *Corey?* To banish her foolishness she spoke quickly.

"Then that's where we'll go. And, ah, what do I call you besides hey boy?"

A bright, winning smile bloomed on the lad's face.

110

"Billy Stilwell, ma'am."

Charity could not keep back the laughter. "Why is it that I think I've been hustled?"

"It is a good hotel, ma'am," Billy hastened to inform her. "Even if my dad runs it."

"I'm sure it is, Billy. We'll get Lucifer and Butch and go to the Republic House."

Charity had decided to pose as a well-to-do young widow looking for investments in land, in hopes that would place her outside the factions involved in the feud. She initiated the first phase of her plan when she checked into the hotel as Mrs. Craig (Moira) Oliver.

"Mister Stilwell," Charity inquired of the man behind the desk, "is there a land office in Longview? Or someone, an attorney or banker, who buys and sells property?"

Stilwell, a man in his early forties, with thinning brown hair and a sparkle in his blue eyes, nodded encouragingly. "Oh, yes, Mrs. Oliver. Most of the land transactions around here go through Bob Carroll at the Timberland Bank. I don't mean to be presumptuous, but was there anything in particular you might be interested in?"

"My late husband, bless him, left an estate of considerable size. Before I left Arizona, I was advised to invest it in real estate."

Stilwell produced a thin, though sincere, smile. "That was wise counsel. I'm sure Bob can help you. His father was in the same profession. He secured title to this land for us so we could build the hotel."

"Thank you very much, Mister Stilwell," Charity answered sweetly.

So much for keeping clear of the feud, Charity thought on the way up to her room. Once established, she set about changing from her travel clothes

111

and arranging her other garments in the curtain-covered closet. She would seek out Bob Carroll the following day, Charity decided.

Bob Carroll was not in his office the next morning when Charity Rose went to the bank. With time to spend, Charity went to the livery. She had seen a nice, fairly new shay the previous day that she thought would add to her pose as a wealthy widow. Riding astride Lucifer would not be consistent with that guise, she decided. After a careful inspection, and some hemming and hawing, she and the stable owner agreed on a price. For an extra forty dollars she acquired a harness-broken mare to pull it. When she called at the bank that afternoon, Carroll had as yet not returned. She decided to take Lucifer out and exercise him.

Over the next few days, with Carroll still not returned from his "urgent business," it became her regular routine to have her shay harnessed early each morning. With a lead-rope on Lucifer, she would trot out into the countryside to put the big black gelding through his paces. On her second afternoon in Longview, Charity went to the office of the bi-weekly newspaper, rather than the busier daily, and ordered calling cards.

She had obtained information of the customs of polite society from a book on social graces she purchased in Fort Worth, during her train ride to Longview. The cards, on stiff white linen paper, were engraved in flawless copperplate script:

Mrs. Craig (Moira) Oliver
Republic House, Longview

Her order called for an immediate interview by a polite young gentleman who wrote the social column. Once she had received the cards, she spent her afternoons, following the exercise session, a bath and

112

light noon meal, distributing them to the homes of the gentry, at the bank and the *Longview Light,* the daily. Her professed interest in land soon brought invitations to tea, dinners, and the admiring attention of the young swains of Longview. By the start of the second week, with Bob Carroll as yet not returned to the bank, "Mrs. Moira Oliver" had acquired a regular couterie of gentlemen in their early twenties, who accompanied her on her exercise jaunts.

Often, these gallants would stage impromptu races of their own blooded horses, wagering large sums. It seemed a delightful way of life to Charity, yet the game had accomplished little, other than to put a heavy drain on her resources. As a lady of "quality," her ears were somewhat protected from such vulgar topics as the progress of a feud, or the identity of the participants. Somehow, she determined, she had to find a way to change all of that.

When the opportunity came, she did not expect it to be the means of opening her horizons. Quite simply, she saw it as only another challenge.

"When are you going to give us an opportunity to see how that black can run?" Peyton Brunnel inquired of her one morning while she worked Lucifer at the end of a long exercise rope.

Instantly intrigued by the idea, Charity quickly considered the proposition. Her sunny smile brightened the faces of the half dozen attentive males who surrounded her, their own blooded stock snorting and blowing in eagerness for that morning's run. Few were thoroughbreds, as Charity had observed before, with stamina and length to their advantage. In this home of the popular Western Quarterhorse, most of the blooded animals were of that strain. Lucifer, a thick-chested Morgan, might possibly take even

113

these, she considered, in a quarter mile race. Even longer, in fact, with a light rider aboard, where the advantage would be reduced for the others.

"Not today, I'm sorry to say," Charity informed them. "You've rested your beasts while Lucifer's been cavorting around this meadow. I, ah, might consider it for tomorrow, though. Say . . . a mile?" Inwardly she hoped with all her being that they'd go for it.

Wry smiles appeared on Brunnel's lips and those of a couple of his friends. "A quarter mile is our usual heat length. What say we stay with that?"

"Peyton," Charity chided, "I declare you're trying terribly hard to take advantage of a young woman. I'd not consider less than half a mile. Lucifer's a desert horse, used to long runs."

"Done," Brunnel readily agreed. "How many entries and what stakes?"

Charity puckered her lips and made a show of evaluating this offer. The pink tip of her tongue flicked along the line of her generous mouth, then retreated. "No more than six, I would say. The field would be too crowded otherwise. And for . . . say, two hundred fifty dollars each winner take all?"

A low whistle of surprise came from one of her admirers. "Such a break-neck course would be entirely too dangerous for a young lady of quality, Moira," Brunnel suggested. "In fairness to you, and your magnificent animal, I'm sure the others would agree to waive our usual rule on owner-riders and allow you a substitute."

Charity exploded with a astonishing smile. "That's too kind of you, Peyton. I appreciate that, I truly do. I'll study on it and perhaps I'll select some young gentleman to ride for me. Right now, however, I feel a demanding urge for a lemonade on the verandah of the Republic House. Are you gentlemen joining me?"

A chorus of "Yes," went the rounds.

Mockingbirds and orioles vied with each other to make the morning noisy. Charity trotted out to the usual field with Lucifer in tow, her spirits high. Seated on the tailgate was young Billy Stilwell. She'd discovered earlier in the week that the boy had a natural affinity to Lucifer and that he was an expert rider, a crucial element in her plan, who had occasionally ridden in stakes races at the county fair and Fourth of July races. Small for his age, 14, he didn't weigh a hundred pounds and should eliminate entirely the handicap a grown man would have represented.

Charity had counted on this when she agreed to the race, keeping open the option of riding herself if her male "sporting friends" disqualified the lad. Either way, she wanted a light load on Lucifer's back. Several of the young gentry had arrived early and greeted her eagerly. Their happy, smug smiles wilted somewhat when they discovered Billy Stilwell would be riding Lucifer. They took it in good strides, Charity had to concede, making side wagers, some of which favored her entry. Billy, Charity noted, was filled with excitement to the bursting point.

"Can we run more than one heat?" he inquired eagerly.

"No, Billy. One will be quite enough. Your jockey's fee should keep you in licorice and jaw-breakers for a year. We don't want to be greedy."

Billy laughed lightly and skipped off into the meadow to look down the course that was being laid out. Charity followed. To her relief, she noted few hazards. A rock outcrop here, some scrub sage and blackberry bushes there. Four trees stood out, spaced far apart and at differing depths into the straightaway. Not bad at all. A quarter mile out, then back. Her fellow entries arrived shortly afterward.

"You mean Billy's going to ride for you?" Peyton Brunnel gasped out.

"He's young, he's a gentleman, and he's ridden before," Charity replied in a tone of calm sweetness. "I believe that qualifies him by the rules?"

"It, ah, does," Peyton reluctantly agreed. "But in an all-out race like this . . ."

"Billy understands the hazards. He's also madly in love with Lucifer. I think you'd have to pry his hands off the reins at this point."

"Places please," the self-appointed steward declared in a loud voice. "All entries to the starting line."

Charity helped Billy into the saddle and the boy walked Lucifer into position with the other entries. A long, tense moment passed, then a revolver cracked and the horses leaped forward. Charity had given Billy careful instructions on the handling of Lucifer and she saw with relief that he had so far remembered them, despite his excitement. Allowing the other horses, accustomed to quarter mile runs, to burn their energy quickly, Billy held Lucifer back, settling into third place and holding position.

With the thunder of the apocalypse, the six blooded steeds whipped past the gathering of spectators and stretched out into a line, noses fixed on the distant flag that marked the quarter mile turn around point. Charity wanted to jump up and down and clap her hands, yet maintained her lady-like poise. With three lengths to the turn, Lucifer had moved into second place.

"Hold him, Billy, hold him!" Charity shouted, forgetting her enforced demeanor.

116

A length and a half ahead, the leader, ridden by Peyton Brunnel, rounded the turn. Clots of sod and turf flew from the flashing hoofs of the straining horses. Billy made it around and Charity thought she could faintly see Lucifer's neck stretch out.

Damn, he'd dropped back a little in the turn and was now in third place again.

"Now, Billy, now!" she cried.

Flat out, Lucifer quickly regained second position. Brunnel's lead closed to a length. To half a length. Billy drubbed the heels of his boots into Lucifer's ribs and kept the whip at the ready. At the eighth mile marker, the two leaders ran neck and neck. Charity made a flailing motion with her arm a fraction of a second before Billy applied the leather tip of his crop to Lucifer's heaving rear haunch.

Lucifer might have taken wings. Ahead by a nose, he churned the ground beneath him as the stalwart black widened the gap to half a length . . . three-quarters . . . then a full length. Brunnel tried gallantly to make up the lost space, but his mount flagged under the strain of the distance. A length and a half in the lead, Billy Stilwell pounded across the finish line.

Charity forcefully restrained her glee as she accepted the stakes and thanked the gentlemen for their contributions. "That's what I call a race," she announced.

"May I escort you to dinner?" came the invitation from three of the excited, hopeful swains.

To which, Charity answered, "Not tonight. I'm taking my jocky out to dine." Beaming widely, a grin spread all across his face, Billy stood beside her and puffed up his chest.

In the days that followed, Charity discovered a change in her status. She remained a lady of quality, right enough, now acquiring a new accolade as a "sporting lady." She was advised of other shrewd wagers and of up-coming races and the young men who had sought her company so avidly before now stumbled over each other to regale her with blood-thirsty tales of the feud. They sought to horrify her and she tactfully allowed them to believe they succeeded. In the process, she learned a great deal.

Two families comprised the core of the feud. The Carrolls headquartered in Longview, as Charity knew. Old Bentbow Carroll, the patriarch, commanded the family's reaction to Wilkes' attempts to run them off their land or organize them into the Wilkes whiskey scheme. Gordon Wilkes, elder of the other warring faction, held court in Nacogdoches. He and his nephew, Dermott, ran the whiskey ring that provided inferior booze for the frontier trade.

In Longview, the county sheriff, Matt Hogan, remained neutral, though was frequently quoted as being "again' " feuding. On the other hand, Frazer McCall was definitely in the Wilkes' camp. Charity learned of the actual "business" at hand that kept Robert Carroll out of Longview. He had been sent by Bentbow to engage the services of Clovis Honeywell, Matt Steadman and Perdanales Pete Rambaud. All three, it was rumored about, had tidy prices on their heads out in West Texas.

Their arrival in town, shortly before the return of Robert Carroll, excited considerable attention. Charity had opportunity to note each of these gents and his habits. She liked none of what she saw. If Baudine and his gunnies rode for the Wilkes, she could see little difference in the trio of hardcases from the Staked Plains. Her realization that she could not bring any of this up without appearing to side with the Wilkes faction kept her silent, and planning.

She would, she decided, remove the criminal element from the Carroll side, which she had come to strongly favor, at a considerable profit to herself when the time came. First, though she had to meet and win the confidence of Robert Carroll.

Chapter 12

Although she had been told a lot about "young" Bob Carroll and his reluctant involvement in the feud, nothing Charity Rose had heard prepared her for a meeting with the real article. Bob was indeed young, younger than some of the would-be suitors who hovered around her. And, she discovered when first ushered into his office, terribly handsome. He stood to welcome her and his six-foot-two height caused her to look up sharply to see his face.

"Good morning, Mrs. Oliver. I'm sorry this meeting has been delayed so long. Please sit down."

"M-Mister Carroll, I . . ." Of a sudden Charity realized she had completely forgotten her alleged purpose in being there.

Captivated by his broad, thick shoulders, open, ready smile, she was reduced to silence for a long moment. Bob Carroll's light brown eyes twinkled and he, too, waited for her next remark. When it came, all artifice had left her.

"Mister Carroll, can I trust you? All I've heard indicates that I might, yet, I . . ."

"Call me Bob, and yes, you can trust me. Only right now I'm a little in the dark as for what and as to why you wish my trust?"

Charity felt compelled to be completely frank. "I—I'm not really Moira Oliver. My name is Charity Rose. I'm here because of the Concho Bill Baudine gang." Quickly Charity laid out her situation and reasons. When she concluded, Bob smiled at her and leaned forward, both hands resting palm-down on his desk top.

"Frankly, I'm less in favor of this feud than you are, ah, Miss Charity. Particularly since my family is involved in it. My grandfather, Bentbow Carroll, sent me to hire those gunmen because some of our faction, the Perkins family, had their three men murdered by night riders I can only surmise were sent by Baudine. At least they worked for Dermott Wilkes. What do you propose we do otherwise?"

"Let me deal with Bill Baudine and his outlaw scum," Charity urged.

"I don't wish to sound condescending, but that's a tall order for a young woman, isn't it, ah, Charity?"

"I've been told that before," Charity responded bluntly. "Before and after I personally dealt with seven of them. All but one of those, who is in jail, are occupying graves, Mister Carroll."

Bob Carroll blinked, tried to produce a smile and then shook his head. "Please, call me Bob. After all I've taken the liberty to use your first name."

"Thank you, Bob. I get the feeling I'm getting through to you, if not quite winning you over."

"Oh, you've won me over, Charity. It's a bit difficult for a man to adjust to the idea of a lovely young woman implacably tracking down outlaws and killing them."

"I collected the bounties, too," Charity informed him. "On them and several others who weren't in Baudine's gang, but got in my way."

"A lady bounty hunter," Bob said wonderingly.

121

"Marshal Joe Carson in Las Vegas, New Mexico, reacted the same way two weeks ago when I claimed the bounty on Lute Waller. I'm accustomed to that, too."

"Remarkable. All right, how would you go about it?"

Charity's smooth, high brow wrinkled as thoughts passed through her mind for inspection. After another weighted silence she nodded as though satisfied and began to lay out her plan. "First off, I'd urge you to go to whomever it took to get rid of those gunfighters. Up to now the Carroll side of this feud has earned the respect and sympathy of many who are not involved *because* you've been the underdogs. The day they arrived here I checked in Matt Hogan's office and there are wanted flyers on all of them. The rewards aren't huge, though together they make a tidy sum. You don't need that kind representing your side."

"Ummm. I can see your point. But in the eyes of other people, what's the difference between them and a lady bounty hunter?"

Charity winced, then produced a smile. "That's a fine line to draw, yet I think I have a suitable answer for all concerned. After Honeywell and the other two are no longer working for your side, I collect the bounties on them and we arrange somehow for the money to get into the hands of the Perkins widows."

Bob slapped a palm on his desk. "You're a ma—er, you've taken a page out my book. I like that idea. We've been, ah, helping them out, but there's only so far a bank can go and keep faith with its depositors. A few hundred dollars would go a long way in these hills."

Now Charity's smile blossomed widely. "It would amount to a little over three thousand dollars, Bob."

"Hell, that's more than we're paying Honeywell, Rambaud and Steadman. I'll get right on it. After that, what?"

"I go after Baudine and his gang," Charity said simply.

"Uh—just like that?"

"More or less, Bob. They have to have a headquarters somewhere around Nacogdoches, right? A small, carefully organized raid on that would take care of their hideout and leave them vulnerable."

"Well and good, only Frazer McCall is sheriff in Nacogdoches and he's so close to Gordon and Dermott Wilkes it's like he's inside their skin. Matt Hogan doesn't have any jurisdiction there."

"He does if we're in hot pursuit. I can go to Nacogdoches, look around and learn what I can. Then we lay a trap for Baudine's men. Once we attack them, chase them there, we have every right to go all the way to their headquarters and finish the job."

"You sound like a lawyer," Bob commented.

"I read a lot of law books when I was a girl," Charity told him. "The point is, there are ways of getting Baudine, if we work hard enough at it. With him and his gang out of the issue, I imagine the feud can be wound down by use of a little common sense."

"Don't be too sure. Dermott Wilkes has powerful friends in Austin. I heard word on the way back here that he's considering going for condemnation proceedings against our property and that of land owners who are backing us Carrolls."

"What does that mean in plain language?"

"The state issues what is called a Condemnation Order, takes our land for a price they set as fair, then turn around and sell it to Dermott Wilkes, or look the other way while he moves in and takes over."

"It doesn't sound honest to me. Or legal for that matter," Charity opined.

"Honesty and legality have little to do with it. Morality even less. It's a power granted to governments so they can build and maintain roadways and the like. It's broadly worded enough, at least the current Texas version, so that unscrupulous men can easily abuse its intent."

"Now you're the one sounding like a lawyer," Charity teased. She found she had rapidly formed a solid opinion of Bob Carroll, based on first impressions and his responses since.

She liked him. As an ally and as a man. His full shock of dark, sandy hair, lack of any facial hair, and rugged build excited something within her. His voice, mellow and with a slight bass rumble to it, soothed her and made her feel comfortable around him. In presenting her case, she acknowledged, she was playing directly to him. Could she be called brazen for that?

"If I do, it's because I am one, in addition to being the bank's property expert. It helps in my work."

"Then why haven't you used it to block what the Wilkes crowd plans?" Charity asked bluntly.

"Their use of legal tactics is relatively new. We have to organize for that. It would help to have someone in their camp who can keep us informed on what and how they're going about it."

Charity nodded eager agreement. "There's another place where I might be able to help."

"How?"

"I'm somewhat in the social whirl of Longview, Bob. Also by racing my horse, Lucifer, I've become an item in the sporting world. A challenge to a Nacogdoches horse or two would get me in down there. The rest I could work out as I went along."

"So long as you avoided contact with this Concho Bill Baudine," Bob told her soberly.

"Ummm. A point well made. Whatever the case, let's get started, shall we?"

Bob nodded and rose from behind his desk. He took both of Charity's hands before he made an answer. "That we shall. Can we do it over a late supper tonight?"

"I, ah, think that can be arranged," she answered lightly.

Redolent with the odors of bay rum, rose water and pine tar soap, Deaver's Barbershop in Nacogdoches did a heavy Saturday morning business. Among the men seated to wait their turn in the chair, Concho Bill Baudine and Frenchy Descoines passed the time by reading the local newspaper. One item, among the list of stage and train schedules, caught his attention.

"Listen to this," he said to Frenchy. " 'The attractive Widow Oliver surprised Longview society last week when she proved herself a fine judge of horses. With a local boy, William Stilwell, riding, she sent her black Morgan gelding, Lucifer, against the best in the county and came off the winner.' That sound familiar to you?"

"Unnh—what?" Frenchy responded, his attention absorbed by a story on land investments in Western Texas.

"A black Morgan gelding, Frenchy. One named Lucifer. Who do we know, a young woman in particular, who has such a horse?" Baudine's eyes glowed.

"The one who hunts us, *non?* This Charity Rose?"

"Right the first time, Frenchy."

"But, Bill, this society lady you read about is

named Oliver."

Concho Bill snorted with impatience. "You've got a better brain than that. Use it."

Frenchy smiled. "She is using a disguise, eh? A false name and pretending to be someone of quality. Why would she do that?"

"I'm not certain, but it doesn't take much to conclude she's after us."

"Of course, Bill, only why in Longview?"

"You've a point. I want some of the boys to go up there and look around. If it's her, I want them to finish her off."

"I'll get them started today, Bill," Frenchy assured his friend and leader.

It had taken three days to convince Bentbow Carroll, *Tatsli* Bowles and Jefferson Monroe that it would be to their advantage not to have the services of the gunhawks they had charged Bob with hiring. The trio had taken the news badly and demanded their entire fee. Bob tactfully talked them into accepting a quarter of the amount and a small bonus. Within half an hour after leaving the bank, they began celebrating in a nearby saloon.

Their hoo-raw went on for the rest of the night and into the next morning. During the process, Clovis Honeywell and his companions learned that it was "the lady horse racer" who had influenced the Carrolls into dismissing them. Perdanales Pete Rambaud's calm indifference got Honeywell to thinking of revenge. By mid-day, Honeywell had gone beyond control. His rage all came to a head when a local barfly glanced the clear portion of the etched glass window of the saloon and casually remarked to another.

126

"There she goes now, that racin' lady and her beau, Mister Robert Carroll."

Charity and Bob had attended a luncheon meeting with Carl Stilwell and Bentbow Carroll. It surprised Charity to discover that the hotelier was a part of the feud, being a cousin of the Carrolls. He had been equally amazed to discover her true identity. The subject of their discussion had been getting Steadman, Honeywell and Rambaud out of town. Matt Hogan had attended also and an agreement developed. After the gathering, Charity strolled along the main street of Longview, her arm resting on Bob's. From the saloon across the street, she heard an angry roar and turned to see Clovis Honeywell rush into the street, gun in hand.

"I'm gonna fix the both of you!" Honeywell bellowed, left index finger pointed at Charity and Bob from the end of his extended arm. "Go for your guns!"

Bob opened his coat to show he was unarmed. It appeared to mean nothing to Honeywell, who swung up his cocked Colt, ready to fire. Five men on the boardwalk half a block away took particular interest in the scene. From the batwings, Rambaud's deep voice spoke commandingly.

"That ain't a wise thing to do, Clovis. Let it lie, I say."

"Back me or keep out of it," Honeywell shouted. Again he brought his gun to bear.

Charity drew her Colt Lightning from under her jacket and shot him in the gun arm. That caused her to blink. It had been a fluke, she'd intended to hit him in the shoulder. The five onlookers exchanged meaningful glances and hurried off. Charity stepped into the street, covering Honeywell with her double-action .38 Colt. She kicked his sixgun away and Bob retrieved it.

"You're wanted in Waco, El Paso and Amarillo, Honeywell. I'm taking you in to Sheriff Hogan. Keep your hands in sight and get to moving."

"My arm's bad hurt, ma'am. I can't keep holdin' it up like this," Honeywell protested.

"Put it where I can see it and we'll get along fine. Now walk," Charity commanded.

With Bob backing her, Charity marched her prisoner to the corner and turned toward the sheriff's office a block away. They neared the alley that ran behind the saloon, when Perdenales Pete and Matt Steadman stepped out into the thoroughfare, hands on the butt-stocks of their sixguns. Rambaud touched his left hand to the brim of his hat, Steadman nodded toward the prisoner.

"Sorry, ma'am, but we can't let you take in our friend," Rambaud informed her.

"You'll have to shoot me to stop it," Charity told him levelly.

Steadman and Rambaud looked at each other. They hadn't considered that possibility. Rambaud, in particular, was reluctant to throw down on a woman, let alone shoot her. While they stood their ground in indecision, the five spectators from the main street gunfight appeared in the mouth of the alley on the opposite side of the street. The weapons they brandished indicated no compunctions about taking on a lady.

"You fellers move away an' we'll finish 'em for you," the leader of the group commanded.

"I don't hold with shootin' a woman," Pete Rambaud growled.

"You want to die with her, yer welcome," came a cold response.

Suddenly angry, Rambaud opened fire on Bill

128

Baudine's gunhawks. Bullets splatted into the clapboard fronts of buildings and everyone scattered for protection. Charity sent a .38 slug through the pelvis of one hardcase, who dived for the protection of a water trough.

He howled in agony and rolled out of sight. Matt Steadman blazed away with his .44 Remington, knocking the hat—and a large chunk of skull—off Les Owens' head. Bob Carroll hugged the dusty street, angry with himself for leaving his sixgun in the office. He felt humiliated, having a young woman protecting him like this. Charity seemed not to notice as she cut down another of Baudine's longriders. Clovis Honeywell lay flat, barely crawling as he inched his way toward the alley, where his friends fought against the strangers. A bullet snapped over his head and he heard a grunt from ahead.

"They got me a good one," Matt Steadman groaned as he sank to his knees. "Help Clovis and get on out of here, Pete. I'm a goner."

"I'll get you out, too, Matt," Pete promised.

"No, too much risk. Wouldn't do no good. Get Clovis."

Horses clattered noisily from the far end of the block. Charity raised up and fired at the approaching man. From the fancy shirt and frock coat, she identified him as Frenchy Descoines. He reined his mount to the right and brought along the horses behind him for his companions. When they came to their feet in an attempt to mount and escape, Charity put a bullet through the right ear of one outlaw.

His blood and brains made a wet spray on the opposite side of his head as he flung sideways and toppled into the water trough. The other two got to their saddles in the confusion and, amid the riderless horses they rushed away. When Charity came to her feet, she noticed that Rambaud and Honeywell had managed to make good their escape also.

"Damn!" she spat. "They got away. At least I can collect on Baudine's men and Matt Steadman."

"Charity," Bob said in an awe-filled voice. "I may not have taken what you said before entirely seriously, but I'm convinced now. Not a scratch on you and you killed two, wounded one."

"That's not the nicest of compliments, but thanks anyway, Bob. Let's get the sheriff."

Ten minutes later, Matt Hogan informed Charity that the rewards would be hers and collected within three days. He also remarked that Matt Steadman left a wife and child, out in Waco. Touched, Charity put a hand on the lawman's shoulder.

"When we cash this bunch in, Sheriff, I want the reward on Steadman paid to his widow, if you'll do so."

"That's mighty kind, Miss Moira, er, Miss Charity. A real white thing to do."

"I don't think I could sleep nights knowing I made a helpless widow and orphan of Steadman's family, Sheriff."

Bob gave her a squeeze. "I'm still shaky from what went on, but I think I'm falling in love."

Charity stood on tip-toe and gave him a peck on the cheek. "Oh, Bob, you say the sweetest things."

Chapter 13

At the top of the hill, the narrow, tree-bordered trail gave way to a wide vista of rolling green hills, dotted here and there with neat, well-tended fields. Bob Carroll stopped the carriage and waved an arm to indicate the vast expanse.

"This is our land," he told Charity. "I love it up here. It's the most beautiful, restful spot in all our holdings."

"I sense its allure. There's something enchanting about this place, Bob."

"I used to come here as a kid, when I had something to cry about and didn't want to cry. I was very touchy about that. So, I'd ride up here and sit under that big pine over there and stare as far as I could see in every direction and tell myself that wherever I went for as far as I could see I could find an aunt or uncle, a cousin or an in-law. This was my kingdom, you see. It's *Carroll* land and no one, especially a Wilkes, is going to take it from us."

Bob's bringing the subject back to the feud sparked a question in Charity. "I've heard the feud being called a whiskey war. Is there much substance in that?"

"Yes, Charity, sadly there is."

"It might help if you tell me. I need to know everything in order to infiltrate their operation in Nacogdoches."

"After this attack by Baudine's men you're not seriously going ahead with that?"

"Of course I am. Not everyone in a city the size of Nacogdoches is insane, any more than they are here. If I get the right connection I can eliminate Baudine and his gang and you can do the rest. Now, tell me about the whiskey."

"We have to go back a way in time for that. Although Sequoia and John Ross, and many of the elders among our people back East came to the conclusion that liquor was an evil thing for anyone, and Indians in particular, the same opinions weren't held by those who had come earlier to Texas under Chief Bowles. In fact, after Austin tried to run all Indians out of Texas, and many Cherokee came to these hills, they began to produce excellent rum from the local sugarcane. Not ones to be highly trusting of governments, white ones in particular, they haven't bothered with licenses and taxes and that sort of thing. In other words, moonshining. That hasn't affected the quality, let me point out.

"Which brings us to now. Dermott Wilkes has some moonshine connections in his family as well. What they'd done with it is to run off one hundred ninety proof alcohol base and shipped it into Indian Territory and outlets along the frontier. There it's mixed with any number of vile concoctions, such as snake heads, plugs of tobacco, strichnine, arsenic, clove oil or other impurities and sold to the Indians and anyone else dumb enough to buy it. It's worked rather well for the folks around Nacogdoches, and now Wilkes wants us to supply him with alcohol base instead of making our traditional rum."

"Whereupon you told him no, I take it?"

"Of course. And ran into trouble when Wilkes' men tried to enforce the idea on people who trace their ancestry to the old Republic of New Fredonia. We're proud people, Charity, and proud of our product. On top of which, we're quite aware of the harm bad whiskey brings to the Indians and consequently the whole frontier. It all began with raids on our stills and quickly spread to killings and now economic sanctions of all types. The idea of condemnation actions is the latest. For some while, since the Perkins family got shot up and robbed, we've suspected organized thieves in on the pickings."

"That's exactly what you've got with Baudine."

"I realize that now. That shoot-out we had in town left me wary. I'll not go anywhere without a gun any more. We need some legal maneuvers of our own. I've considered organizing all our ground under one entity, call it, say, the Fredonian Land Development Company."

Charity took on an expression of eager interest. "That sounds like what you need. If the land involved was all under lease or ownership by this big company, you'd have a lot more clout than a few individual farmers, trying to fight the system."

"That's it, exactly. Politicians as a class are probably no less honest than any other group. Yet, a lot of the bad ones sure seem to get caught often."

"True. By then it's too late for the poor victims of their schemes," Charity added. "What you need to do is get it stopped up front. I think your development company is the ideal solution. While you're doing it, you need to get people to band together to provide mutual protection."

"That's already being taken care of. Jeff Monroe and *Tatsli* Bowles are organizing a company of the

133

Light Horse. It's the traditional Cherokee police-cum-militia. They've asked me to captain it."

"That's marvelous, Bob. Now, tell me, are you too traditional to kiss me?"

Her open invitation astonished Bob Carroll. For over a week he had found himself strongly attracted to Charity, yet the immediacy of their problem kept him at a distance, unable to express his feelings. After a brief, initial hesitancy, he took her swiftly into his arms and covered her lips with his.

Charity pulled him tightly to him and shivered at the insistent probe of his tongue. She ran a hand down his broad back, thrilling to the ripple of muscles and the heat radiating from him in a sudden rush. Her breathing roughened, her chest resounded to the pounding of her heart. With one hand, Bob cupped her left breast and began to knead it. She sought his shirt front and started to unbutton it. Bob moaned softly and let her tongue follow his back inside the warm cavern of his mouth. When their embrace ended they could only gasp and stare avidly at each other in the intensity of their passion.

"It—it jus-just got s-s-started," Charity gasped at last, aware of her hand on his bare chest.

"Don-don't let it stop now," Bob pleaded.

"I won't . . . I can't . . . I don't want it to stop, ever."

"Not here," Bob cautioned when Charity began to undress. "There's a spot, up under that big, old pine."

Bob took a blanket, Charity a half gallon fruit jar of lemonade. The scent of tingly pine pitch excited her ardor as she breathed deeply under the low-hanging branches. Quickly she revealed herself to him. Bob studied her long and thoughtfully, back-grounded by a screen of fuzzy light, shining through the long pine needles. Then, slowly, he removed his clothes.

His smooth, bronze skin glowed. Charity gasped at the size of his aroused organ. Timidly she stepped close to him and cupped his firm flesh in one delicate hand. Bob shivered and took her by the shoulders.

"You are so lovely. So delicately beautiful," he told her in a low, uneven voice.

Charity trembled as Bob bent low and kissed her up-hilted breasts, drawing the nipples to rigid readiness. Bob's kisses continued, down to her navel, lingered, then progressed. Charity groaned with the intensity of wild sensations.

Moving awkwardly, she spread her legs to give him easy access. Bob knelt before her and took her buttocks in both hands. Pulling toward him, he buried his face in the frilly folds at the gate to her aching passage. In frantic abandon, she began to thrust her pelvis against him.

"Oooooh! Bobby! She shook and writhed and tossed her head from side to side, exploding again and again as he drove deeper and more insistently into her cavern. When she thought she could endure no more sheer, nerve-jangling delight, he ceased abruptly and turned away from her to spread the blanket. Then he drew her down with him and positioned her on one side.

Lying against her silken flesh, Bob crackled with the sublime joy of their contact while he maneuvered into position. Slowly, watching intently while her eyes went wide and blank, he entered her. Charity went wild with the overwhelming mixture of pain and pleasure. Never in her limited experience had she encountered such as this.

Charity's movements became frantic and uncontrolled until they rolled over, with her on her back.

She locked her legs around Bob's narrow waist and began to drive him into her, blind to all but that unbelievable joy his repeated contact with her gave her.

With a heave he tilted himself and she trembled with renewed bliss. Then . . . then . . . then . . . Swirling rapidly upward to the pinnacle, they joined in a mutual shout of delirium as they burst over the peak into the downy, warm, surge of the eternal sea. Tiny cries and utterances of ebullience sighed from their lips and they lay still.

"You've . . . been saving up for a while," Bob observed after a long, sated rest.

"Yes . . . I have. So, it seems, have you, Bobby."

"I, ah, never liked that name as a kid. But, when you call me Bobby, it comes out just right."

"I've . . . I've never, never known a man so . . . capable of thrilling me through and through. I . . . oh, Bobby, it was wonderful."

"You astonished me, too." A throaty chuckle followed. "This is the second time I've been surprised in this very spot."

"Oh?" Charity managed to ask archly. "When was the first one?"

"It was my first time. I mean, the first ever. I suppose every town has its early bloomers. Longview had Mary Sue Jelkey. The story that went around to the boys was that Mary Sue would accommodate anyone who asked her. She was sixteen, I was thirteen. Well, I asked her and, much to my surprise and confusion, she said yes.

"She laughed at me, giggled really, and said a little twerp like me wouldn't do much good but I'd learn a thing or two and probably enjoy it. So, we came up here. Next thing I knew she had her hand in my pants. That felt pretty good. At least she didn't try to yank it or pinch it off, like another girl I'd come close to taking advantage of. We came out here, her giggly, me all eager, and excited, and scared. Real scared, it turned out, when we got here. She said, 'Well, lets go.' And I thought she meant turn around and head back. Then she laughed and squeezed my crotch and climbed down from behind me on my horse. She had her dress off before I knew what was going on.

"I was real scared, all right. I'd been up there to the point of aching and sure I'd split the skin open if something didn't happen. Now it went right down. Limp as my grandmaw's noodles. I got all embarrassed, didn't even want to take my pants down. Mary Sue solved that for me. She saw how little and limp it was and dropped to her knees.

"Things got real wild after that. She, ah, she did what seemed right to come next and went to work. Before long I was inflated again. Only now Mary Sue wasn't making jokes about not being able to find it. I might have been a little guy for my age, but not *all* of me. So, right here, I got the surprise of my young life when I found out I had a commodity much in demand and could do a whole lot with it even if embarrassed and scared half out of my mind. Mary, uh, Mary Sue she got surprised too. She even said she wanted to come back the next day. Sort of help me learn the hows and wherefores."

"Did you?"

Bob grinned foolishly. "Shouldn't I have?"

"This is one of their largest still operations," Concho Bill Baudine informed the seventeen men waiting in front of him in a semi-circle. "And it's damn near on the Rusk county line."

"Which means?" Bert Clay asked.

137

"If we get in a jackpot, we don't have to ride a quarter mile to be in Nacogdoches County. I'm sure you know that once there, the law will see things our way, no matter what happens. Now, listen carefully. Once we get within a mile of the still, we split up into three groups. We'll come at them from the north, west and south, which puts their backs against the hills. Try not to harm the cooker and the coils. Bust up the fermenting vats and aging barrels. Set fire to the house, barns and cane press. Any questions?"

"Who's in charge of the other two groups?" Bert inquired.

"You'll ride with Frenchy, the other group will be led by Ike Tremble," Baudine informed him.

"What if they show resistance, instead of scatter like usual?" Lane Burkette asked.

Concho Bill produced a wolfish grin. "Kill 'em all. Anyone else?" When he received no further queries, he tightened his reins and turned his mount's head. "Let's move out."

Indistinct images flitted through the screening trees and underbrush. The briefly glimpsed shape of a hat and head, the muzzle of a horse, the broad, straight line of shoulders and back telegraphed to the watchers the presence of their enemy. Tension became an almost palpable thing. Bob Carroll raised in his stirrups to ease his own anxiety-cramped muscles, and glanced around.

"They're comin'," he whispered to those closest to him, slipping into the easy vernacular of the hill people. "No doubt about it now."

"We're ready," Anson Monroe responded. "We'll whup 'em good."

Bob looked closely at his twenty-year-old cousin.

138

"Don't be too eager, Anse. They've got more bullets than we've got riders. Remember that. Pick your targets and take your time. We'll trail along and hit 'em right before they split up."

"How you know they're gonna split?" Martin Gal-chaser queried.

"You know of any other way they can hit Bill Monroe's still and get away with it?" Bob gave him back.

"Uh . . . no. Don't reckon I do."

"Then, let's be ready."

Ten minutes later the approaching hardcases halted abruptly and arranged themselves into groups of six. Concho Bill raised his arm to give the signal to head out, when the air filled with cracks and moans and the pop of discharging rifles came from all around his men.

"Ambush!" Malcolm Evers shouted. A moment later blood spurted from his left shoulder. "I'm hit!"

"Let's get outta here!" Lane Burkette yelled in panic.

"Hold tight," Baudine commanded. "Close up and hit one place only."

Whirling in confusion and firing blindly, the out-law band milled about, churning up dust and old leaves, before forming into any semblance of a cohesive unit. Then, at Baudine's signal, they charged back along the track they had followed.

Howling after them, the Light Horse gave chase. Once clear of the timbered hills, Baudine's men scattered, each seeking a route that would take them back into Nacogdoches County. The Light Horse steady closed ground. Bob Carroll and five of his militiamen came within twenty-five yards of four longriders as they splashed through a shallow stream and up a sloping bank to a meadow beyond. Fingers

139

of orange flickered as the pursued men opened fire. Immediate shots answered them and one hardcase threw up his arms and fell from his saddle. Then half a dozen mounted figures appeared from a hedge line and blazed away. One heavy slug shattered a tree limb, which dropped across Bob Carroll's shoulder and his horse's neck, unseating the young man.

Bob fell as the others raced on. Slightly wounded, and facing a far superior force, Anson Monroe called to the others to turn around. In the wild, early dawn melee, they missed sight of Bob Carroll, lying in the tall grass. Not so Sheriff Frazer McCall. When he and his small posse trotted forward with Concho Bill Baudine and two of his men, Bob, groaning, had just sat up.

"Well, Bob Carroll," Sheriff McCall observed sarcastically. "You over-played your hand this time. You're under arrest for murder and assault. I'm taking you in to Nacogdoches."

Chapter 14

Loudly jangling, a bell burred through the lobby of the Republic House in Longview. Carl Stilwell answered the electric summons and spoke into the telephone instrument.

"Republic House. Who's calling?" He paused while a voice crackled over the wire. Carl's face drained and he next spoke in a hollow tone. "What was that, again? Bob Carroll's what?"

"Been arrested," the distant caller assured him. "He's in the Nacogdoches jail."

"I—I'll get right on it," Carl promised, hanging the one-piece device on its hook. "Billy!" he called to his son.

Word of Bob's arrest went around quickly, especially to the Carroll clan. Bentbow Carroll and Jefferson Monroe met and the rallying cry went out to the hills. For the first time, a serious mobilization began of the tough, fiercely independent dwellers in the country south of Longview. Charity abandoned entirely her assumed persona and made no effort to conceal her partisan support of the Carrolls.

"Bob was saying that we had to use legal means as well," Charity declared to Jefferson Monroe the second day after Bob's arrest. "What he did was acting in defense of property. Can't we take a lawyer down there and get him out?"

Jeff Monroe shook his head sadly. "Not to Nacogdoches, we can't. The judge down there wouldn't listen."

"Isn't there some way?" she urged. "There has to be someone who'll not side with the Wilkes faction."

Lips puckered, Jeff considered the situation. "There might be one way. Bob was on middling-friendly terms with Treavor Wilkes. He's a good attorney, despite being a Wilkes. They thought alike about the feud. Couldn't abide it, in other words. If someone could talk to Treavor . . . Ah, but that's out of the question. Gordon Wilkes will have someone watching every man around here."

Charity brightened. "You said the magic word. Every *man*. A woman could get through relatively easily. I'll go see Treavor Wilkes."

Jeff frowned. "It'll be dangerous."

"No more so than staying around here. The place has become a powder magazine. Longview people who aren't siding with the Carrolls have organized a vigilance committee to see the violence is kept out of town. All of your hill people relatives are armed to the teeth. Before we knew it, the whole place could go up."

"Like I said, it could be mighty dangerous for you. The folks down Nacogdoches way have their dander up, too. Strangers will be viewed with suspicion. They've got 'em a real, live Carroll to hang and they're not likely to give him up easily."

"All the same, I'm going," Charity announced.

Two days later, following a brief morning thunder-shower, the noon-time southbound stage rolled into Nacogdoches. Aboard were a returning, repentant wayward husband, a firearms drummer, a whiskey salesman and Charity Rose. Charity had given no name and traveled in the clothing of a style favored

142

by women some twenty years her senior. She had added cornstarch to her auburn locks, combing it in artfully to give her a touch of age. Long, fingertip to elbow gloves concealed the telltale youthfulness of her skin, as did a heavy veil and a cosmetic which bleached the ruddy glow of her cheeks to an aged pallor.

Affecting to have laryngitis, she spoke in a high, breathy manner to further aid her disguise. To her relief and satisfaction, her arrival went without particular notice. She dispatched a small, single bag to the Lone Star Hotel. Then she started out to walk along the main street, back slightly stooped, her weight borne on her furled parasol. Few of the idlers or busy shoppers gave her a second look. Three blocks down, she paused to study a small white sign suspended under the overhang of a balcony.

TREAVOR TRAVIS WILKES, ESQ.
Attorney at Law
Upstairs

Following the arrow's indication, Charity went to the end of the building and climbed the stairway attached to the outside. She rapped lightly on the door, which had a top panel of frosted glass, then entered.

"Good morning," a severe-looking woman of indeterminate age said from behind her desk. "May I help you with something?"

"I'm here to see Lawyer Wilkes," Charity informed her.

"Did you have an appointment?"

"Ah, no. I do hope he'll see me, though. It's terribly important."

"Your name?" The forbidding secretary withdrew a brown lead pencil from the roll at the base of her up-swept bun of hair.

"Is — is that necessary? What I want to discuss is only for Mister Wilkes."

"If you are to speak with Mister Wilkes, he'll have to know your name."

"It's, ah, Megan Quincannon."

"Very well, Miss Quincannon. It is Miss, isn't it?"

"Yes."

"Mister Wilkes is in court right now. The noon break should be coming any time now. I'll let him know you're here."

"Thank you so much." Charity took a seat, an uncomfortable, unpadded, straight-back chair, and studied the pattern in the wallpaper. Twenty minutes went by, while the secretary consulted handwritten notes and pecked at the keys of a shiny new, Underwood typewriting machine. Charity had about reached the conclusion to return the next day when the door opened and a slender, handsome young man entered.

He had an aura of self-confidence and the small graceful gestures of a person accustomed to command. He wore a conservative suit and a narrow brimmed white Stetson. He dropped his hat on a hat tree and greeted the secretary.

"You're overdue for your lunch hour, Miss Williams. Why don't you go now?"

"Thank you, I will, Mister Wilkes. There's a young lady to see you. A Miss Quincannon." She gestured toward Charity.

"Oh, all right. Treavor Wilkes, Miss Quincannon. Won't you come in?"

Charity entered Treavor's inner office and took the far more comfortable chair he offered. The interior had been tastefully decorated with a solid, masculine theme. An antelope head adorned one wall, along with a rack containing two expensive, foreign-made double-rifles. There was the ubiquitous spitoon, por

144

traits of the president and the governor of Texas, along with the national and state colors. A large humidor of tobacco and a rack of pipes graced the desk, along with a leather-bound blotter and an ink well.

"Now, may I ask your reason for consulting me?" Treavor inquired after taking his own seat.

"This is a little out of the ordinary. First off, my name is not Quincannon, that's my aunt's name. I used it for, ah, convenience. I am Charity Rose, I'm a bounty hunter and I'm here to apprehend Concho Bill Baudine and the members of his gang. They are all wanted in Arizona and New Mexico Territories and in several counties in West Texas."

"And why do you need a lawyer to do that, Miss, ah, Charity?"

"I don't. If that were all there is to this." Charity took a deep breath and launched into her situation, asking her first impressions to be valid. "Baudine and his men are in the employ of Dermott Wilkes, as enforcers for the Wilkes side of the feud with the Carrolls. Robert Carroll is in jail here in Nacogdoches, charged with murder and assault. I'm here to get a lawyer to represent him. He didn't murder anyone. He, and those with him the other night, acted in defense of their lives and property, and in another county. Put simply, the Carroll family needs help. That's why I came to you."

"You are aware that there might be some, ah, conflict of interests?" Treavor returned with a hint of a smile.

"I'm also aware, on the advice of Jefferson Monroe and Bentbow Carroll, that you are, or were, a friend of Bob's."

"I see. My present infamy with the family had preceded me. What is your part in this, ah, feud?"

145

You say your name is Rose?"

"Yes. My involvement is partly personal. Bob and I are, ah, close. Also, I must admit to being a partisan of the Carroll faction in this matter. It's their land and their crops and an attempt to force them into acceding to another person's wishes as to what to do with them is against the law. I heard that you are a fair man, a gentleman of mild manners, with a successful law practice. Who better to appeal to?"

Treavor chuckled low in his throat and ran long fingers through his curly blond hair. "You've certainly piqued my interest, Miss Charity. The trial I'm involved with is in recess until tomorrow morning. That gives us time to go over this matter in detail. But first, let me offer you lunch."

"That's most generous. I'm only just off the stage."

"And no doubt absolutely starved. I know the food at their waystations rather well. We have a professional men's association here in Nacogdoches, doctors, lawyers, judges and the like, with our own private club. It would be my pleasure to escort you there," Treavor offered gallantly.

"I'm delighted," Charity responded, reflecting that Treavor lived up every bit to his advance billing.

They had quail, a brace of open-fire roasted birds each, with cottage fried potatoes, stewed greens and small, individual English trifles for dessert. Along with the repast came suitable wines and a rich, aromatic coffee with the pastry. Charity ate her fill and they talked of inconsequential things. At last Treavor returned to the subject at hand.

"I heard of Bob's arrest and questioned its validity at the time. Although, without a client, there was little I could do."

"You have one now," Charity answered, laying a hand on his.

"We'll return to my office, you can give me a retainer and we can get started. The first stop will be the jail, to visit Bob and get the details of his arrest."

"You had better do that one alone. Frazer McCall is, ah, known to be friendly with Bill Baudine and the, ah, Wilkes family."

"What you mean is that my grandfather owns him."

"Well, Treavor, you said it, not I."

"It's true, Charity, I'm sorry to say." During the meal they had progressed to a first name basis and handled it with ease.

"The point is, if Baudine finds out I'm here, the results could be bloody."

"You can wait in my office," Treavor offered.

An hour after Treavor departed, leaving Charity to browse through his law books, he came back, looking troubled. Without preamble, he launched into a summary of what went on.

"McCall didn't even try to hide it. He's aware of what those Light Horse riders were up to. Also that Baudine was involved. All the same, Bob and a couple others crossed over into Nacogdoches County and McCall arrested Bob. Which, needless to say, delighted my grandfather. McCall's not about to turn Bob loose without a fight. Or a court order. Judge Simpson is having a tooth extracted this afternoon. That's why we're recessed until tomorrow. I'll probably not be able to get this before him until Motions Session on Monday morning. Even if Judge Simpson does grant Bob bail, there's nothing saying he won't be bound over for trial." Charity frowned and Treavor answered it with a wry grin. "Even then I have a trick up my sleeve."

"What's that?"

"I can put in for a change of venue and have the

trial continued to the next session. Which happens to be called for Longview."

Charity brightened. "That works right to Bob's advantage, doesn't it?"

"It does that. Of course, the county prosecutor and Sheriff McCall will fight like the devil to prevent it. All the same, we'll see what happens. In the meantime, I don't feel it's safe for you to remain here. I'd suggest you return to Longview and come back in time for the bail hearing."

"It . . . might be best," Charity relented.

Treavor Wilkes escorted Charity to the stage the next morning and saw her off. Some ten miles north, near the Nacogdoches County line, Concho Bill Baudine learned that a woman who might be Charity Rose had been in Nacogdoches, raising a stir about Bob Carroll's arrest. He sent men to town and others to check out the stage.

Isaac Tremble and Bert Clay decided that checking on the stage might as well be a profitable endeavor. They laid plans accordingly. When the coach slowed at the top of a steep downgrade that sloped to the river, five men jumped the guard and driver. Three heavy slugs cleared the shotgun rider off the seat, spraying his blood on the driver.

Rather than giving in, the gutsy, bearded coach-man popped his long whip over the rumps of his six-up teams and released the brake. Immediately, the Concord coach lurched forward and careened down the road. Rocking and bouncing, it gave a fearsome ride to the passengers. Charity Rose managed to keep enough control to remove a Colt Lightning from her large brocaded purse. Across from her, a young man hung on with one hand and produced his sixgun. Of one accord, they pulled back the leather curtains and began firing at the desperados.

A bullet snapped past Malcom Evers' head and caused him to reflexively flinch away, which put his head in position to come in contact with a leg-thick branch of a hickory tree.

His combined velocity and the stoutness of the limb turned his head into a soft, broken bag of mush. Unmastered, his horse galloped wildly away, the raw scent of human blood heavy in its nostrils. Frank Harker rode in close to the coach in an attempt to end resistance. His familiar, leering features registered on Charity's brain a moment before she double-actioned two rounds through her .38 Lightning.

"Franny!" Frank Harker's close friend, Bert Clay, shouted in warning a moment before the back of Frank's head detached from his skull and struck Bert in the face.

"B'God, we didn't come out here to get killed off," Pete Emory shouted to Ike Tremble.

"Yer right, Pete," Ike agreed with a bellow. "Let's haul outta here. Way I see it, that damned Charity woman's sure's hell on the stage and not a lick we can do about it."

"Bill ain't gonna like it," Pete observed as they slackened speed and let the noisy coach bound roughly away over the rutted road.

Ike produced a grim smile. "Reckon I'll have to answer for that."

Chapter 15

Heavy, black thunderheads, their huge, anvil tops crowned with silver light, towered over Nacogdoches the next Monday when Charity arrived again on the stage. Once more she affected the disguise of an older woman. Bright flashes and deep booms sounded as the celestial display warmed up for a regular deluge. It produced an awesome, somber mood for the ordeal she and Bob would soon face. Treavor Wilkes looked up smilingly from his desk and greeted her.

"It went smoothly this morning. We're to go before Judge Simpson this afternoon at one-thirty, for bail to be set and a hearing on the change of venue."

"Which means?" Charity inquired, a bit out of breath.

"By two o'clock, Bob could be out on the streets and on his way back to Longview."

"From the crowd in the street, I'd say word got out about what you planned," Charity observed unhappily.

"I'm afraid so. In our system of law, the courts are open, you know. I don't like it, but there's little we can do."

"Someone talked in Longview, too," Charity responded. "There's likely to be a number of folks here to see what goes on."

"That could complicate matters. All we need is a shooting war right in the center of town." Treavor frowned and indicated the papers on his desk. "I'm preparing my brief for the change of venue. It should be simple enough, but no guarantees. We need to get over there in about an hour, so little time left. I'll keep at this and you get rested and something to eat."

"I don't think I could eat right now," Charity told him.

"Do so anyway. An appearance in court can be an awful strain on the system."

"If you say so," Charity answered simply.

An hour and ten minutes later, Judge Aubrey Simpson heard his clerk read off the case pending and looked up with surprised eyes to see a Wilkes standing before him, representing a Carroll. Treavor Wilkes began his presentation, speaking low and forcefully, making each point telling and precise. His excellent argument for the release, at a modest bail, of a Carroll further astonished the jurist.

"Since it is the defense's contention, your Honor, that my client acted in self-defense, bail is not inaccessible even though the charge is murder. For that reason, and the aforestated causes, I request bail be set in the sum of one hundred dollars."

"Mister Prosecutor, do you have any argument to be heard?" Judge Simpson inquired, peering over the upper rims of his spectacles, which had slid to the tip of his nose.

"I certainly do, your Honor. The whole idea of bail is ludicrous when it comes to a matter involving a principal leader in a bloody feud, such as this individual."

"Objection, your Honor, that hasn't been proven,'

Treavor injected.

"If we let him out of here, that'll never be proven," the county prosecutor snapped.

"Gentlemen," Judge Simpson warned with a light rap of his gavel. "Let's hear Mister Proctor's argument without further interruption, then you may answer to it, Mister Wilkes."

"Very well, your Honor."

Prosecutor Proctor proceeded to outline all sorts of terrible crimes that might occur if Bob Carroll were allowed to walk the streets again. In conclusion, he added; "Besides, if he's let out on bail, Gordon Wilkes won't be the least bit happy."

Rising to the challenge, Treavor took the floor again. "What my grandfather likes or dislikes is of no importance here. The law is. My client is entitled under that law to make bail, and there's nothing you have said to the contrary that stands the test of veracity, to prevent it. We don't *know* he'll become a danger to society. We don't *know* that he might seek revenge on the persons of Gordon or Dermott Wilkes, or upon Sheriff McCall. We aren't even certain at this point if the hand that held the gun, which took the life of Les Owens, was in fact Robert Carroll's. But we do know that Les Owens was a member of a group known as the Concho Bill Baudine gang, who are wanted in Texas, New Mexico and Arizona for various crimes, from murder and bank robbery to rape and cattle rustling. We know that Robert Carroll is an attorney and a banker and has a home, an occupation and property in a neighboring county. He'll not fail in meeting the obligations implied and stipulated by bail. The law is clear. Robert Carroll is entitled to bail. I ask that one, as low as possible be fixed, your Honor."

Judge Simpson considered this powerful appeal a

short while, then rapped his gavel. "Bail is set at one hundred dollars. What am I to hear next?"

"Argument on my motion for a change of venue, your Honor," Treavor spoke up. "First off is a most pragmatic reason. This trial we're currently undertaking will run over-time for this session. You know that, your Honor, and the prosecutor has already admitted so in open court. Which means there can not even be a preliminary inquiry during this session. My client is entitled to a speedy and public trial. It will be six months before this court sits in Nacogdoches again. There's nothing 'speedy' about that. Since that is clearly the case, and particularly since he has been granted bail, shouldn't the entire matter be held over to the next immediate session and tried then?"

"Anything else, Mister Wilkes?" Judge Simpson asked dryly.

"There's ample precedent for the change of venue, and I've cited the cases in my brief, which I'll give you for consideration. Beyond that, there's a human factor to consider. In my honest opinion, taking into consideration that I am a Wilkes and know my family well, I have strong, serious doubts that my client can receive a fair trial in this county."

"See here, what sort of poppycock is that?" County Prosecutor Proctor blurted.

"If that's an objection, it's over-ruled. If it's not, keep your mouth shut," Judge Simpson snapped. "The rules on that apply equally to both of you. Now, have you more, Mister Wilkes?"

"No, your Honor."

"Mister Prosecutor?"

"I can only reiterate that if we let this murderer out of our jurisdiction, we'll never see him again. He's been identified as the leader of some vigilante organization known as the Light Horse. That alone should put him in insurrection against the sovereign State of Texas. If the accused can't get a fair trial here, what sort of fair hearing will the prosecution get in Longview? Lastly, a required court appearance two counties away for our sheriff would put an undue strain on proper and adequate law enforcement in this county. Thank you, your Honor."

"I'll read your briefs and consider what has been said here, the demeanor of the accused, and other aspects, and render my verdict in an hour. Court is in recess until three o'clock this afternoon."

"All rise," the bailiff called out.

"Well, did we win or lose?" Charity inquired when she rushed forward.

"Honestly, it could go either way," Treavor told her.

"He's only saying that, honey, because I'm a lawyer, too," Bob teased her.

"Well, I sure wish it had ended right now. I'm starving," Charity announced.

"Didn't you eat?" Treavor inquired, surprised.

Charity looked down, like a little girl who'd lost her doll. "I couldn't. I got too tensed up. Now I could eat a whole cow."

"We've got an hour. Why don't we all go?" Treavor suggested.

Outside, a large crowd had gathered. Rumor had it that the Carroll-Wilkes feud might be getting settled inside. Representatives of both factions mingled easily for the first time in eight months. Some even shook hands and exchanged news of their latest rum production. When folks among them recognized the trio at the top of the steps, their murmur of conversation turned to a roar.

"What's going on? What's happening?" came the repeated questions.

"We won't know for half an hour," Treavor Wilkes replied. "Let us through. We want to go get something to eat."

"Tell us the news," several insisted.

"What's the judge say?" queried several others.

Compelled to force their way through the throng, Charity and the two men at last broke free and headed for the seclusion of Treavor's private club.

"It don't look good, goddamnit, it don't look good at all," Dermott Wilkes growled to his grandfather.

"What did you do to stop it?" Gordon Wilkes demanded.

The sixty-year-old patriarch of the Wilkes faction sat in a wooden rocker on the porch of his large ranch home outside Nacogdoches. His thick thatch of curly hair, the black shot through with salt-and-pepper, blew in the breeze. One large hand tightly clenched a pewter tumbler, beaded with condensation, which contained the dregs of a mint julep. He breathed with effort, his rock-hard bulk seeming to make his movements ponderous. His dark eyes glittered with intelligence as he waited a reply.

"Not damn-all I could do. Simpson agreed to hear Treavor's case . . ."

"Damn that boy! He's a traitor and a disgrace to the name Wilkes. We—we're family. I held him on my knee when he was a little shaver, same as I did you. What took him to do this?"

"A woman they say," Dermott blurted out, immediately regretful he'd not withheld his bit of gossip.

"*What* woman?" Gordon demanded.

"Someone Baudine claims to know. A female bounty hunter who had thrown in with the Carrolls."

"Carroll. Damn the name. We'll wipe them all

155

from the face of the earth. Get me Baudine. I want something planned to bring an end to all this."

"Yes, sir, Grandad. Right away."

"It is the decision of this court," Judge Simpson intoned at three-oh-five that afternoon, "that, in order to meet the law's requirements for a fair trial, in addition to one that is speedy, that a preliminary inquiry into the elements of this case shall be heard by this court one week from today, in Longview. The county prosecutor is advised to prepare all evidence and arrange for all witnesses to be present at that time. At that time, Mister Proctor, you will be ably assisted by the county prosecutor of Harris County. This court is adjourned."

"You did it!" Charity exclaimed ten minutes later in Treavor Wilkes' office, relief coloring her words.

Charity, Bob and Treavor had left the courthouse by a side exit, avoiding the crowd out front. All the while, the young attorney maintained a troubled expression, which didn't depart which they reached his chambers. Her elation notwithstanding, Charity noted this and queried Treavor.

"We've won, yet you look like it was the end of the world. Why?"

"We've only won the first round," Treavor explained. "The hard part is yet to come. Starting with getting Bob out of here safely. You two should be on the next stage, and I'll be with you."

"Won't that be rather rubbing it in the family's faces?" Bob asked.

"I did that when I stood up for you in there, Bob," Treavor acknowledged.

"Which I deeply appreciate. My point is, using a few technicalities to get me out on bail and such is

156

one thing. Your grandfather's likely not to see this sudden departure for Longview by his, ah, 'wayward' grandson in quite the same light."

"That I'll have to worry about if and when it comes along. For now, let's be ready to take that night stage."

Treavor Wilkes created a sensation by his clever maneuvering. More than he had expected. All of East Texas vibrated with talk of the up-coming trial. At the center of the tempest, Charity and Bob went about seemingly oblivious to the stir they had created, which others avidly nurtured.

During the week before the first hearing, they attended parties, rode about the countryside and made sweet, delicious love. Only the frequent presence of Treavor Wilkes, with his incessant questions about the night of Bob Carroll's arrest, reminded them of the ordeal yet to be faced. When the day at last arrived, Longview had more than doubled in population, or so it appeared.

Members of both factions had traveled to the city and lined the streets outside the courthouse. In order to protect both parties, Judge Simpson ruled that only accredited journalists, clergymen, and members of the two boards of county commissioners would be permitted inside as spectators. That would, he declared, serve to inform the public well enough. In a surprise, unprecedented move, Treavor Wilkes requested of the court that all witnesses be removed and kept in another location until summoned to testify. In addition, he asked for a court order prohibiting those who had been heard from discussing their testimony with others yet to be called.

Judge Simpson mulled over this unusual set of

conditions, hesitant to create a precedent that might later be successfully challenged. On the other hand, were he to rule in favor of the defense, and it later became established procedure, he would be hailed as a brilliant, far-seeing, jurist. In chambers, Treavor Wilkes argued eloquently.

"Judge, under the present system regarding witnesses, how many times have you sat on the bench and listened while one witness after another told the same story, word for word, chapter and verse? It goes for defense, as well as the prosecution. For instance; although the man in question was guilty as sin, he is alibied by three witnesses who, using the *exact same words*, testify that at ten o'clock, the hour of the murder, they sat down to play cards with the defendant. They remember it, they say, because the clock in the courthouse steeple chimed the hour. They also recite the first poker hand each man held. The accused goes free, only to murder again before he is at last convicted and hung."

A smile spread on Judge Simpson's face. "The State of Texas versus Chambers, a year ago. In Nacogdoches, as I recall. I heard both cases. You've made a good point, Treavor. Let's go back in and I'll rule."

From that point the hearing went easily. One witness after another paraded onto the stand. Treavor was merciless in his cross-examination, yet presented nothing by way of defense. When Proctor concluded, attorney Wilkes made a short summation of the defense position. Judge Simpson retired to deliberate. Out in the street, feelings ran high.

Some of the privileged few who sat in the courtroom managed to get information to the gathered crowd. What they heard heartened many. Enemies of a day ago exchanged handshakes. Carroll supporters bought drinks for men in the Wilkes faction. The feud, they speculated openly, appeared to be over. An electrifying wave passed over the throng when word went out that the judge had returned to court to make his decision.

"As to the first charge, of deliberate murder, the prosecution has failed to support the burden of proof to the satisfaction of this court. I will come back to this point in a moment," Judge Simpson announced. "Now, on the lesser charges of assault, mayhem and trespassing, I'm reducing the assault and mayhem to disorderly conduct, a misdemeanor, and dismissing the trespassing as pernicious prosecution."

Startled exclamations from the observers interrupted Judge Simpson. He banged his gavel for order and glowered at the politicians and newspaper men. "That will be quite enough. I might," he tried for humor, "have expected such an outburst from Mister Proctor, however I must insist the decorum of this court be maintained. Now, as to the gravest charge, that of murder, there is a provision under the statutes for a lesser offense. It is the view of this court, after examining the evidence and testimony, that sufficient cause exists to try the defendant for involuntary manslaughter. I made that decision partly on the defense contention that the defendant acted in self-defense. It is my feeling that, for the best interests of all parties, the matter should be aired in open court. The defendant is to be bound over for trial, bail remains in effect. This court is adjourned."

A swift, chill breeze, harbinger of another thunderstorm, swept through the street outside, when Charity, Treavor, and Bob appeared at last. Most of those present had turned up collars and added heavier garments. They saw nothing unusual in Charity wearing a large fur muff on a bright, sunny day. The threat of cold rain to come explained a lot of things. A ragged cheer roused from both factions. Bob and Treavor turned slightly to shake hands and the roar of approval grew louder. In that instant, a bullet snapped past Charity's ear and she instinctively jerked her head to the side, in time to see the slug strike Treavor in the throat.

"Treavor!" Her scream came too late.

Chapter 16

Stunned silence fell following Charity's shout of alarm. Immobilized by shock, the onlookers gaped at the falling man and at Charity who yanked away the muff, to reveal a Colt Lightning, as she turned to face the assassins.

Three of four men at the front of the crowd, weapons in hand, broke to run to safety. The last one had not even taken a step when the Lightning cracked and a bullet burned through his left temple and scrambled his brains. Before he fell, Charity lined up on another of the murderers and squeezed off two fast rounds.

Bits of cloth, blood and flesh flew from the running killer's back as hot lead smacked into him. A pink froth appeared on his lips as he fell face-first into the stones of the street. At once, Charity turned for another shot.

Others joined her now. Weapons came out in both factions. A voice shouted from the back of the crowd.

"The Carrolls killed Treavor Wilkes!"

Another took up the contrary cry. "Them Wilkes' took a shot at Bob!"

Of her last three rounds, Charity felt certain at

161

least one had struck meat on one of the fleeing pair. So far she seemed to be the only one moving fast in a world of slow motion. Then a bullet cracked through the air only inches above her head and she let go the empty Colt Lightning, to draw the second from her shoulder holster. Hunkered low, she scanned the area, looking for the hidden assassin. Around her, pandemonium began as others started to react.

More shouts came, accusing she and Bob of killing Treavor. Angry men started their way and Charity stood up, gun in hand, to face them. Her peripheral vision caught a blur to her right a moment later and Bob tackled her as another blast came from the unseen gunman.

There, her mind recorded as she toppled to the stone steps. Second floor window of the hotel. From down the block she heard more gunshots as Carroll followers engaged the fleeing killers. The face she had seen registered at last. Lane Burkette. Concho Bill Baudine had to be behind the attempt to kill all three of them. The sniper's rifle barrel barrel appeared again and Charity fired first.

Her slug sheared splinters from the edge of the window casing. Reflexively, the gunman jerked backward, elevating the muzzle of his weapon as it discharged. A fraction of a second later, flames began to eat at the flimsy curtain material. Tendrils of smoke streamed from a broken pane and the crackle of the fire grew louder. Someone noticed it and shouted over the crowd.

"Fire! The hotel's on fire!"

Glass tinkled and the window facing the courthouse shattered from heat. Flames leaped out from the room and began to eat at the clapboard siding. The immediacy of this emergency ended hostilities. Former grievances forgotten, the men close by yelled for buckets and several ran to notify the volunteer fire department. Bob took a tight grip on Charity's upper arm.

"Let's get out of here."

"Treavor . . ."

"It's too late for him. Once that mob gets the fire under control, they might turn on us. We'd be better off out in the hills."

Charity cast a regretful glance backward at the pathetic disheveled pile of clothes that marked Treavor Wilkes. A large, darkening pool of blood surrounded the fallen man.

A loon called hauntingly from the pond behind the big log house where Concho Bill Baudine made his headquarters. Baudine sat alone in the kitchen, the dishes from his supper still on the table. He rose and poured another cup of coffee as the door opened and Frenchy Descoines entered.

Frenchy no longer appeared the dapper, stylish dresser. His coat had been torn and soiled, his shirt sodden from perspiration. Dirt and smudges of greasy powder residue streaked his attire and face. He also bore on his cheeks and chin scabs of dark, crusted blood where splinters had struck him. With a heavy sigh, he sank into a chair.

"Where are the others?" Concho Bill demanded.

"Dead. Lane Burkette and the other three. That damnable Charity Rose killed two of them and the mob got Burkette and Grimes."

"What about Carroll and Wilkes?"

"Treavor Wilkes is dead. At least I think he is. I shot him through the throat. Bob Carroll and Charity Rose got away."

"How is that? How can five of you, from no more

than twenty or thirty feet miss two people?"

"It's a long story and I'm tired, *mon ami.*"

"You'd better get rested fast. I want you to tell Gordon Wilkes what happened. A version that will insure he sees it our way."

"In the morning, eh, *mon cher Guillaume?* I need a drink, something to eat and a long sleep."

Inconsistent with the way he ragged his other men, Bill Baudine agreed to Frenchy's request. William Baudine and Maurice Descoines went back a long way together. All the way to the New Orleans orphanage where they had been raised. Bill Baudine had protected the younger, smaller Maurice from the physical and sexual abuse of some of the other boys and certain staff members. When he, himself, could no longer endure the torments of that place, Bill Baudine ran away. He set up a series of petty crimes, which netted more money than he had expected, then went back for his friend.

Close as brothers, they had pursued a life of outlawry from that time on. The deep fondness each held for the other transcended many flaws which neither would have tolerated in others. Concho Bill prepared a meal for Frenchy, saw he had a glass and bottle of whiskey then bid him good night. Early the next morning they rode to Gordon Wilkes' main ranch.

"What have you come to tell me?" big, bear-like Gordon Wilkes growled. "It can't be anything good, from the looks on your faces. Get on with it."

"I'm sorry to inform you, Mister Wilkes, that your grandson, Treavor Wilkes, has been killed," Concho Bill stated in a forced tone of regret.

"That can't be. He might have turned his coat on us, but he hasn't been involved. No reason for that."

"It's true, all the same. An act of treachery on the

164

part of the Carroll faction," Baudine assured him. "They have hired a female bounty hunter, named Charity Rose, who fired the fatal shot on the steps of the Longview courthouse."

"No! I won't believe that. He was working for them," the huge man, who suddenly looked old and haggard, insisted.

"Something must have gone wrong. This man was a witness. He saw exactly what happened," Baudine came back, indicating Frenchy.

"*Oui, M'seu* Wilkes," Frenchy took up earnestly. "I was on the street and saw it. She drew a pistol from hiding in her muff and shot young Treavor in the throat. He died almost at once. A terrible thing."

Don't stretch it too far, Concho Bill thought urgently.

"What is your name, young man?" Gordon demanded of Frenchy.

"Descoines, *m'seu*. Maurice Descoines."

"Uh—well, then, Mister Descoines, although I'm saddened by this news, I thank you for bringing it to me. I'll have to consider this for a while. Stay around the home place, Mister Baudine and I'll convey my wishes to you later today. Now, please excuse me."

Dismissed in such a manner, their backs turned as they walked away from the veranda of the main house, Concho Bill Baudine and Frenchy Descoines didn't see the tears that formed in Gordon Wilkes' eyes and ran hotly down his lined cheeks. Shortly after the noon meal, Gordon Wilkes sent for them.

"I need the name and description of that woman. I'm putting a thousand dollar price on her head and five hundred on Robert Carroll. Dead, not alive. I'm also going to personally oversee the destruction of the Carroll faction and all they own. I'll inform my grandson, Dermott, of this and from now on, you'll report directly to me, Mister Baudine."

"Yes, sir."

After their departure from the Wilkes home place, Concho Bill spoke seriously with Frenchy. "I want you to get the word out and gather all the boys. I don't like this much now. We're going to have to gather up all the loot we can and be out of here before someone sorts out the whole mess and comes after us."

"You two are hotter'n a bunkhouse cookstove," Jefferson Monroe informed Charity and Bob. "Most folks don't know which way to turn any more. We were lucky to get that fire out at all. Worse, it left a bunch of armed Wilkes supporters in control of the town for the first time ever. Even those not on our side, some of the town vigilance committee, ignored that to fight the blaze. Now they're stuck with it and the Wilkes crowd are stayin'."

"We had nothing to do with the shooting. Treavor being alive at all is a miracle. Don't the town people and your faction know we're innocent?" Charity asked with a sinking feeling.

"Sure, some of 'em do. Thing is, you ran out, which makes Bob look bad, and those who ran with you are more than willing to put the blame on him instead of face up to it. It's human nature."

"We've done nothing wrong. Not even when I shot Les Owens," Bob protested. "What can we do to make it clear we had nothing to do with the shooting?"

"Not much I can see, Bob," Jeff replied. "Best thing is for you to stay out of sight, out of people's way until Treavor either recovers or dies. Then you can have your say and people will listen."

166

"Where should we go?" Charity asked, her thoughts wistfully on Dos Cabezas.

"Up in the hills. To *Tatsli* Bowles, I'd recommend," Jeff suggested.

"I feel like we're running away again," Bob said resentfully.

"We aren't," Charity told him. "Even if it seems like we are."

Birds twittered in the oaks, hickory and pines. Here and there squirrels scolded cheekily as they kept jealous watch over their precious acorn crop. Sunlight, softened by the leaves it filtered through, made dappled patterns on the bright blankets spread in a circle around a large, old, hand-hewn chair placed in the position of honor. Each family group, divided according to their clans, sat on and around the woven robes. After the circle had been purified with sage smoke, a wizened old man, his face a ravaged gulley of wrinkles, rose and spoke.

"Let them speak for themselves and then we will decide what we can do."

Robert Carroll stepped forward first. He faced the ancient one and lowered his head in a symbolic bow to authority. "*Adawa'hi wado*. Thank you, Wise Man," Bob repeated in English. Then he turned and addressed the general clan meeting. "You know me. Many of you have grown up with me from childhood. You know I do not speak lies. The *unegage'ya*, Charity Rose, did not shoot Treavor Wilkes. I stood at his side when the shot was fired. It came from the hotel, the same window where the fire started. Let's be settled on that one thing before more is said. I have spoken. *Wado*."

"*Quaquu Uwoyeni, wado*. Thank you, Bob Hand.

167

Are there those who would speak?" the aged man asked.

Several did, the majority supporting Bob. When the last had expressed his feelings, the old chief motioned for Bob to continue. What he had to tell them came from long discussions with Charity. Their determination to see the hill folk reorganized into a reliable fighting unit came from the certain knowledge that their opponents, and the neutrals of both Longview and Nacogdoches would be more inclined to see reason when faced with superior force.

"You must be prepared," Bob summed up his argument. "Anyone here can tell, if they take a careful look and think about it, that the terrain and situation decree that any strike by Wilkes forces, or anyone else, will probably come first at *Tatsli* Bowles' farm. We need everyone to agree and to stand ready to ride at an instant at the sound of trouble. No one from outside is going to fight for you. You must do it for yourself, and for your neighbor. The Light Horse, under *Timi* Monroe, will continue to patrol. What we need, what *you* need, is to organize for pitched battles. I think it's coming to that, so does Charity, so does *Tatsli* Carroll."

"So does *Tatsli* Bowles," *Tatsli* called from the audience.

Polite laughter followed. Their interest fully engaged, Bob went on with his plans. In an hour the meeting concluded in a jovial round of feasting and dancing. Late that night, the men of the clans rode home with their assignments and life returned, somewhat, to normal in the hills. *Tatsli* Bowles, of all the families represented, took his responsibilities most seriously.

First off, like Bob, he knew his farm would most likely be hit first in any attack. Secondly because of his life-long desire to live up to the significant and symbolic name given him. *Tatsli* meant First Frog of Spring in Cherokee, and had been the name of a legendary warrior and close friend of Chief Bowles, *Tatsli*'s ancestor, who established the Cherokee Republic of New Fredonia in Texas long before the coming of the Americans. *Tatsli* Bowles would prepare for war, and with him would be Charity Rose and Robert Hand Carroll.

Forty men rode north with Gordon Wilkes. Their number included his grandson Dermott and his workmen, Concho Bill Baudine's remaining sixteen outlaws and, incongruously, six newly arrived Texas Rangers. With the evidence of a severely wounded, unconscious man, the Rangers had accepted the Wilkes version of the incident. So far, Dermott and Concho Bill had managed to keep it from Gordon that Treavor was not in fact dead. Consequently, the old man sought a terrible vengeance.

He would have it, too, it appeared, as they moved unopposed into Carroll country. Ahead, in a fold of the hills, lay the *Tatsli* Bowles farm. Stands of pine, hickory and oak dotted the rising terrain. An eerie silence seemed to precede the riders so that as the wooded heights enclosed them, they heard nothing but the pounding of their horses' hoofs. Beyond a sharp turn in the narrow trace they followed, they came upon a large field of corn.

"Not far now," one of Dermott's men, who had scouted ahead, informed Gordon Wilkes.

A bleak smile creased the face of the Wilkes patriarch. "Have the men ride down this corn. Break the stalks, kill it all off. Then we go on."

Twenty minutes later, their destructive task completed, the vengeful posse started off. A large clearing in the thickly wooded section could be discerned ahead when they covered a quarter mile. Gordon Wilkes ordered the men to spread out and advance at the ready on a wide front. Frenchy Descoines came upon the first of the opposition, chopping down a bee tree.

Before the man could cry out, Frenchy hurled a thin-bladed knife with consummate accuracy It pierced the man's throat and prevented any warning cry. Frenchy dismounted and retrieved his dagger, which he wiped clean on his victim's shirt, then returned to the saddle. Another three hundred yards brought the posse to the edge of the treeline. Dismounting at a silent order, they took careful aim on the spacious log house and tidy barn beyond a small creek, and opened fire.

Chapter 17

Bullets slammed loudly into the thick shake shingles of the Bowles house. Built originally as a small, tight log cabin, it had been added onto with the advent of prosperity and the coming of more children. The original had been intended as a fortress, this later version had not. Glass tinkled in the windows as the posse poured a steady fire from across the creek.

Shouts of alarm came from the Bowles women as they ducked flying glass and lead. *Tatsli* Bowles, who had been in the harness shed when the firing began, grabbed up a long-barreled goose gun and returned fire, scattering leaves with the first two charges, then he reloaded with buckshot. The heavy pellets began to chew up the underbrush on the far side of the creek. Yelps of pain followed from slightly wounded men.

Charity Rose heard the firing and realized at once she was trapped in the barn. She'd come to care for Lucifer and thanked whatever providence had caused her to leave her .45–60 Marlin Pacific in the saddle scabbard. She drew out the big rifle and took a position at one of the side windows. The booming discharge of her weapon gave serious pause to several of Baudine's men who were preparing to wade the creek and close in.

Their sudden retreat caught Charity's attention and she quickly aligned her sights on one of the outlaws. Struck between the shoulder blades, his arms flew wide and he buried his face in the soft, black mud of the far bank. His companions didn't even slow down to retrieve his body. The respite gave Charity time to wonder where Bob might be.

Crouched below the sill of a second floor window, Bob Carroll took careful note of the positions of their enemy. From his elevated location he could see the hats, and often the shoulders, of the men across the creek. Satisfied he had located those who constituted the greatest threat, he opened up on them.

In the explosive noise of Bob's fusillade, three of Dermott's men died, shot through the head or chest. It brought instant retaliation. Only to be responded to from an unexpected place.

With a slap of wood on wood, the door to the outhouse opened and a light rifle barked twice. Under cover of the smoke and taking advantage of the surprise his shots had created, young *Quida'* Bowles ran for the kitchen door. His father's voice bellowed from the equipment shed.

"Peter, get to the house, damnit!"

Quida's feet drove puffs of dust from the hard-packed ground as he sprinted to the porch and dived through the door, held open by his little sister, *Elini*. Moments later his small thatch of black hair, tinted auburn in streaks by the sun, appeared at a window and he opened fire once more.

Fully six hundred rounds came from the besiegers over the first half hour of the battle. They had plenty of ammunition, Charity decided, and weren't shy about spending it.

"Some of you men get upstream," Concho Bill commanded. "Ford the creek and come in behind them. Start setting fire to the buildings if you can, then we can shoot 'em when they come out."

"There's women and kids in there," Ike Tremble protested. "I ain't much on shootin' them."

"Leave that to the Wilkes'," Baudine told him. "Feuds don't take much account of age or gender."

Over the past quarter hour the fighting had slowed down to occasional sniping from both sides. After Baudine sent his men off to cross the creek, he took stock of the area that was his responsibility. Whoever was in that barn, he reasoned, had to be a damned good shot. He'd lost two men and Wilkes three more to the marksman who never showed up at the same place twice in a row. A sudden thumping of galloping hoofs and a flurry of shots to his right attracted the gang leader's attention.

Three large men, barrel-chested, black-haired and well armed, dashed their horses into the farmyard from the woods beyond the house. One ran to the barn, the other two to the house. Bullets kicked up dirt beyond them and one slug parted a clothesline. Their arrival brought another fusillade from the defenders. If they didn't finish this thing fast, Baudine considered, chances were the whole countryside would be down on their necks.

"There's a lot more of them than us," Charity explained to *Tomi* Bowles, the eldest of *Tatsli*'s family. "I'm in favor of withdrawing before they get around us and hit from another direction."

"And let them burn this place?" *Tomi* growled.

"Dad would never go along with that."

"We may not have a choice. If we stay we could die here and they'd burn it anyway," Charity reasoned.

"You've a point. There should be more people on the way here. We were over the ridge or we'd been along sooner," *Tomi* informed her.

"Your father's in a vulnerable position. Tell him in your language that we'll give covering fire and for him to make a break for the barn."

Liquid syllables of the nearly sung Cherokee language sounded clearly across the farmyard. A moment later, the door to the harness shed opened. Charity and *Tomi* blasted at the enemy, rapidly levering through full magazine tubes. Little return fire answered them. What did went wide of the mark. *Tatsli* Bowles stomped into the barn, puffing slightly, eyes alight with his eagerness for battle. He grew indignant when Charity explained her view of their predicament.

"There may be a lot of them but we're better shots," *Tatsli* snapped.

Tomi gave Charity an I-told-you-so look. A moment later, bullets slapped into the opposite end of the barn, verifying Charity's prediction.

"We're caught in the middle," *Tomi* declared.

"Can't stay here," Charity agreed. "We should let the horses free and get to the house."

"Those bastards'll burn my barn," *Tatsli* snarled. He headed for the long side of the building opposite where Charity stood.

Bullets punched through the wooden walls. One struck an iron wagon tire and moaned off in the dusty air. *Tomi* went to join his father. Her weapon reloaded, Charity kept up a steady fire on their enemy across the creek. The rapid crack of five weapons beyond the barn increased in volume. Suddenly *Tatsli* Bowles cried out and slumped back against a stall side.

"Dad!" *Tomi* yelled.

"They got me good, son. You're in charge of the family now. Always do what you think right."

"No, Dad. We'll get you out of here," *Tomi* protested.

"Not alive, you won't," *Tatsli* responded in a liquid gurgle. He shuddered, went rigid, then collapsed.

"Well, *Tomi*?" Charity asked.

"You were right. We've got to get out of here."

"And away from the farm," Charity urged.

Again *Tomi* used the Cherokee tongue to advise the defenders in the house. He and Charity released all of the horses and chased them out the rear door. Then, when a barking volley came from the house, they flung open the front door and ran from the barn to the back of the house.

Ike Tremble waited three minutes after the heavy firing ceased before he led his five men to the barn. He found it empty, except for the dead man, and he issued terse instructions to the others.

"Set this place afire and we'll move on to that tool shed. After that, the harness room, chicken coop and last the main house. Bill says to leave the killin' of the woman and kids up to the Wilkes bunch."

"All right by me," Bert Clay answered eagerly.

"Don't hold with that sort of doin's, either," Zeke Walton added.

"Set a good blaze, boys. I'll cover the back," Ike prompted.

"We shoulda brought along some popcorn," Buck Stoval quipped.

"Don't be a wise-ass," Ike growled.

"They've fired the barn," Bob Carroll announced from the top of the stair.

"Time for us to be moving," Charity stated.

Dry-eyed, *Waleli* Bowles nodded agreement and gathered her children. "They'll destroy this place," was her only comment.

"I'll lead the way," *Tomi* Bowles offered.

"And I'll bring up the back," Bob Carroll volunteered.

"I'll help you," young *Quida* Bowles put in.

"No, son. Your father is already dead. We don't want to lose any more."

"Awh, Mo-o-om," Peter pouted.

"He can be of help," Bob suggested. "He makes a small target and he can shoot well."

Two minutes later, while thick, black smoke rolled over the yard from the barn, a final blaze of fire came from the house. Then those inside raced out into the covering billows and off toward the thick woods behind the farm. *Waleli*, Charity and the little Bowles girls made it, behind *Tomi* and his brothers. Then the men setting fire to the harness and tool sheds completed their tasks and looked up to see the retreating figures.

At once they opened fire. Not before Bob Carroll managed to drop one of them with a bullet in the heart. Lead flew wildly. Ducking and running, Bob and Peter dashed for the protection of the trees. A slug cracked past Bob's head and another split a fence post to his left. He turned in his headlong dash and emptied the magazine of his rifle at their pursuers. Once again he started off.

Fumbling as he ran, Bob reloaded his magazine. While he did, Peter stopped behind a small young

176

elm tree and provided covering fire. When he heard Bob stop, he began to run. The small, slim boy made six running steps when a powerful force clouted him in the hip.

Quida cried out in pain, stumbled and fell. Bob started for the lad, but bullets kept him pinned down. Peter began to crawl, dragging himself by his arms. At that moment, the first of the outlaws drew near. He fired without pausing, putting a slug into the back of the boy's head. Roaring his outrage, Bob Carroll stepped from cover and put four bullets in Buck Stoval's twitching body before the gunman hit the ground. Blinded by tears of fury and grief, Bob trotted after the other refugees.

In the distance, behind, he heard a ragged cheer and the tinkling sound of breaking glass. A moment later dogs began to bay. Spurred on by this, Bob closed the gap and caught up to the escaping family.

"Where's *Quida?" Waleli* asked anxiously, eyes wide with the dread of foreknowledge.

"Dead," Bob burst out in a sob. Then he recovered his emotions. "It's my fault. I had him stay behind. I avenged him on the man who did it. We've got to hurry. Wilkes has set dogs on us."

The fugitives turned from their aimless progress onto a boar trail through the woods. Bent low in many places, they put more space between them and those who sought their lives. When two of the game paths intersected, *Tomi* Bowles chose the other one and switched over. *Waleli* bent low with a large tin box and began to sprinkle bright orange, cayenne pepper in all directions from the crossing. The longest stream she left along the course they followed.

"The dogs are getting closer," Charity panted.

"The pepper will stop them," *Waleli* said with a grim grin.

How can she stand it? Charity wondered. Husband and youngest son killed by criminals in less than an hour and she goes on like this was a picnic outing. In her experience, only the dreaded Apaches had such strength and resolve. What a remarkable people these Cherokees were. The baying of the dogs grew much louder and men's voices could be discerned.

"Faster," Charity urged in a whisper. "They're nearly on us."

A moment later, more voices came from directly ahead.

"They've trapped us," Charity hissed.

For a moment she felt panic, then a cold resolve to take many of them along when she died. She saw a sudden flash of gray-black at the corner of her vision and turned to fire, only to find Butch at her side. Perhaps Lucifer had escaped, too. No time for that, Charity concluded. Any moment now they would be overwhelmed.

Chapter 18

Not a bird nor squirrel remained in the area. All the small animals had gone to ground. Inexorably the voices came closer from front and rear. Then one, louder than the others, hailed from ahead.

"O'siyo' Anitsalagi'!"

Immediately the Bowles family, and Bob, relaxed and rushed forward. Three men waited at the closer edge of a large clearing. They waved and quietly greeted the survivors of the fight. When the news had been given of *Tatsli* and *Quida'*, and a rundown on their pursuers, the leader of the relief force directed them to quickly cross the meadow. The reason immediately dawned on Charity.

"This makes a good place for an ambush," Charity remarked to Bob and the leader of the new arrivals, *Denili* Monroe.

"Right you are," Daniel Monroe assured her with a bloodthirsty leer. "We're going to get every one of them."

"We'd be better off to capture them. There's been enough killing," Charity urged. "With them as our prisoners, the law can step in and bring an end to it all."

"They have the law with them," *Denili* replied.

179

"We've been scouting their positions and saw the Texas Rangers. They will not listen to us."

"Sheriff Hogan will," Charity tried again.

"Maybe. I have forty men here, hungry for revenge. I'll ask that they spare those who give up. The others will die."

When the chase reached the intersection of trails where the pepper had been spread, Concho Bill Baudine motioned to his men and they held back. Doggedly the others, led by their baying bloodhounds, continued. In no time, the animals began to howl, squawl and paw at their noses. Baudine nodded knowingly and signaled his men with a jerk of his head.

Once away from the interrupted pursuit, he spoke quietly. "Too much chance of getting turned into the quarry out there. While they go after the women and kids, let's go back to that house and empty out the valuables."

"Good idea, boss," Zeke Walton agreed.

With their dogs useless now, the Wilkes men spread out and advanced over a wide area. One of them encountered the correct trail, some five hundred yards from the clearing and called the others to him. He pointed forward and hailed the first to come into sight.

"They went that way, must be trying to circle around us."

"Won't get away with that," Gordon Wilkes growled. "I'm gettin' tuckered, boys, but sight of them Cha-roggies'll get my dander up again. Keep a'movin'."

"The Rangers went back for their horses," Dermott Wilkes informed his grandfather.

"Maybe they can cut 'em off from the other way," Gordon answered in satisfaction.

At the edge of the clearing the posse halted again. Audrey Wilkes, a cousin of Dermott, pointed to the bent and discolored grass.

"They went through there. Must have been scared not to cut around the sides, and leave marks like this. Let's go after them."

Half way across the three hundred yard meadow, the edge of the woods erupted in streaming puffs of smoke. The sound of the shots reached the posse nearly as fast as the bullets. Three men fell and wild fighting broke out. Bits and pieces of tree limb and leaf floated downward from wild rounds, while the exposed Wilkes faction ran frantically to find cover.

Certain that wholesale slaughter would not solve the feud, Charity held her fire, content to act only in self-defense. To her relief, Bob did also, though he frequently put a shot close to one of the retreating posse to hurry the man along. From the far side she heard the gravelly voice of Gordon Wilkes.

"Pull back! Pull back! They must have half the county hiding in there."

Five tense minutes followed, then the six Texas Rangers rode into the meadow. "Hold your fire! All of you, cease firing!" their sergeant commanded. "Texas Rangers. Hold your fire!"

He waited, gun in hand, while both factions complied. Then, quite slowly and without any sign of fear or uneasiness, the sergeant rode toward the tree line where the fugitives and their rescuers waited, weapons set to fire. Once he had passed beyond the outer screen, deeper into the trees, the defenders began to show themselves. Squint-eyed from years in the hot Texas sun, the sergeant peered around until he recognized Bob Carroll from a description.

181

"Are you Bob Carroll?" he asked. "Sergeant Jesse Millard, Texas Rangers."

"I'm Carroll," Bob answered. "Did you come to arrest me, Sergeant?"

"Not exactly. Which one is Charity Rose? She's wanted for murder in Nacogdoches, reward posted by Gordon Wilkes."

Charity stepped forward, despite Bob's effort to prevent it. "The only men I killed in Nacogdoches were assassins. By now, I expect Treavor Wilkes is dead. They're the ones who shot him at the courthouse. They were members of the Concho Bill Baudine gang and I have a right to the bounties on them."

"Ummmm. Treavor Wilkes isn't dead yet, Miss," Sergeant Millard informed her. "His grandfather believes he is, and chances are he will die. The old man swears he has a witness who saw you shoot Treavor. That's why the reward."

"No way it could have been me. I carry a pair of Colt Lightnings, in thirty-eight long Colt. Those men of Baudine's were armed with forty-fours or forty-fives, I'm sure."

"That's no help, I'm afraid, Miss," Millard revealed. "No slug was recovered. Even checking the wound channel would be of little use, because they don't run true to caliber. And a doctor could only do that if there was a corpse to work on." Sergeant Millard thought a moment and spoke in an easier manner. "I'm familiar with the wanted flyers on Baudine and his men. You say they are here?"

"Yes, Sergeant Millard. In fact you probably rode out here with them."

Scarlet color darkened Millard's face. "One doesn't expect wanted men to be riding with a posse. Of course, that doesn't excuse me not recognizing them.

You're certain they're working for Wilkes?"

"Oh, positive, Sergeant. I saw Frenchy Descoines in Nacogdoches the day Treavor was shot."

Now far greater discomfort assailed Sergeant Millard. "*Frenchy* Descoines, is it? I'm afraid to admit what an idiot I've been. Gordon Wilkes told me that his witness was a Maurice Descoines. I, ah, never made the connection."

"Now that you have, what about us? What about ḣat wanted poster?"

"I, ah, I'll see what I can do about having it lifted. The best bet is for you to turn yourself in. That way your cooperation will be noted officially. While everyone waits to see what happens to Treavor Wilkes, my men and I can look into the Baudine involvement."

"Absolutely not. If we're put in custody in Nacogdoches, the door to the cell won't even be closed before a lynch mob has Bob and I out under a tree limb. We're staying around Longview."

"What do you propose as an alternative?" Sergeant Millard inquired.

"An armed truce. Like you said, we have to wait to see what happens to Treavor. If he recovers, he can swear that I did not shoot him. If not, we'll have to figure out our next step at that time."

"A truce, eh? An *armed* truce? Why's that?"

"We want some assurances that we'll not be attacked by the Wilkes bunch again."

"All right. For how long?"

"Like you said, until Treavor recovers. Or dies."

Late springtime brought a special laziness to the Texas hill country. Barefoot boys, many shirtless, some with breech cloths instead of denim trousers,

183

flocked to favorite fishing spots and swimming holes. The green corn would be ready for a special festival soon, Charity was told. The unsteady truce labored along as she settled into hill life and found it to her liking. The cool nights and warm, invigorating days appealed in a special way, her being a desert dweller, and the abundance of water and rainfall astonished her. Two days after the battle, she and Bob moved in at Evan Monroe's holding, at the urging of *Denili* Monroe.

To her great delight, when she arrived, Lucifer was there to whinny a greeting. He had been rounded up on the morning after the attack at the Bowles farm by shy, undersized, twelve-year-old *Gayo'tli* Mason — whose name Charity discovered meant uncompleted, and who had been born prematurely. Gratefully, Charity rewarded him with a five dollar gold piece, a foot-long stick of horehound candy and a big hug. The boy had the size and physical development of a child four years younger, but he idolized Charity and followed her everywhere. Except, of course, when Bob was present.

Charity and Bob spent a great deal of time together. Most days, a steady breeze made a soft soughing through the tall pines and restless hickories. When Bob wasn't busy with other duties, he and Charity would walk or ride out under those stately boughs and talk of the old times.

"More than fifty years before the Mexican government opened Texas to settlement by the Americans, Chief Bowles and representatives of nearly every clan of the Cherokees came here," Bob told her. "Contact with the whites during colonial times had not always been the most pleasant of experiences. After the founding of the American Republic, quite a few Cherokees, who had 'gone white' discovered their

English-born neighbors to be suspicious, unfriendly and covetous of their land. An unfortunate shooting scrape, labeled the 'Mussel Shoals Massacre,' by the whites precipitated events, so they answered the call of Bowles and moved out, bringing their families, farming equipment and slaves to Texas. Later a white court cleared the Indians who'd acted in self defense and helped the survivors reach New Orleans.

"Chief Bowles called his settlement the Republic of New Fredonia. Towns and plantations were established, some in the European manner, others according to Indian custom, for many tribes had representatives here, including all the five civilized tribes, the Kickapoo and many others. The coming of white homesteaders, and the eventual conflict between Mexico and the Texicans, brought an end to the noble experiment. Then, when Steven Austin betrayed Sam Houston's trust with the Indians of Texas, our ancestors scattered. Many went to Indian Territory, where by then, the land-hungry whites had removed the rest of our people."

"It's such a sad story," Charity observed. "For a people to be pushed out and pushed around for no stronger motive than greed."

"It's what's going on now," Bob enlarged. "Dermott Wilkes wants to make a lot more money. He figures he can do it by taking what is ours for his own use. That it's the Indians getting pushed once again has nothing to do with it. In fact, some of those backing Wilkes are of our people."

More often their conversations were far less philosophical. They talked of the birds and animal life and of rum making and what this rich, verdant land could become in the future. And they talked of love.

By Wednesday, Charity sensed that Bob's involvement went far beyond lust or infatuation. Her own reactions were mixed, and unclear to her. As she lay in Bob's arms that afternoon, she tried to form words to express her feelings and describe their relationship. She found them hard to come by.

"Bob, over the short time we've been acquainted, we've become quite, ah, intimate," she tried by way of broaching the subject.

"Ummm, you might say that," he concurred as his finger traced the raised nipple of her firm right breast.

"I'm trying to be serious, Bob," Charity returned. "We've got to think about the future."

"Ummmm. That's what I'm doing right now," Bob answered as he raised himself on one elbow and warmly kissed her rising nipple.

"You're outrageous, *Quaquu Uwoyeni* Carroll," Charity yelped.

"Oh-ho! So you've taken time to learn my Cherokee name, eh? That means we're in love."

"More likely in *lust*, Bob Carroll, from the feel of what I have in my hand." No more able to long maintain a serious mien than Bob, Charity broke into a fit of throaty chuckles.

Slowly she began to stroke his upright manhood, while his lips explored her body. Fine tendrils of chilling delight radiated through them, growing in intensity with each ecstatic moment.

"Aaah!" Bob exclaimed at the first touch of lips and tongue to his sensitive flesh. "Something you learned out at those, ah, Tanks, with your little friend, er, Corey?"

"His name was Corey, yes. And you're a beast for bringing him up at a time like this."

"Well, I'm curious," Bob defended. "Curious about everything that's a part of you. C'mon, tell me. Was it Corey?"

Charity growled at him and shaped her short, well-formed nails like claws. "Yes, darn you, Corey taught me. He—I—we . . . both liked it."

"As do I, beloved. You were doing fine. While you're at it, I think I just might . . . ummmmmm-mmm."

"Oooooooh! Bobby, Bobby, that's so marvelous."

Then she stopped speaking to deliver her gratitude in a far more graphic way. Soon the pulse of creation surged in both of them and their heated bodies blended into one set of euphoric sensations. Shivering on the tenuous edge of dissolution, they ceased their energetic loving and Bob lay on his back. Charity quickly straddled him, willing the exquisite sensations to last until new pleasures replaced them. Slowly, her face closed in concentration, sea-green eyes glazed, she impaled herself on his magnificent device.

A keg of cannon powder could have exploded beside them and neither would have recorded the event. Deliriously involved, they became one with nature and the universe, as they swayed, rocked, thrusted and retreated. A curious jay alighted on a branch above and dislodged a leaf.

It floated downward in a lazy spiral, to land on Bob's chest. At its gentle touch, Bob exploded into frantic completion, drawing Charity in with him to a whirlpool of release.

"Rider coming!" *Gayo'tli* Monroe called out in a thin, high voice.

Friday morning had brought a light rain, which did little beyond settle the dust. Bob Carroll and *Denili* Monroe came from the still house and Charity Rose left the corral to discover who might be bringing news. Don't let it be bad news, Charity thought fiercely. Their visitor turned out to be Sergeant Jesse Millard, the Texas Ranger who had arranged the truce.

"Howdy, folks," Jesse greeted, a smile raising the wide, thick sweep of his mustache. "Thought you might enjoy hearing some good news."

"That would be a change," Bob Carroll replied dryly.

"Is Miz Bowles here?" Millard asked.

"No," Bob informed the Ranger sergeant. "She and the children are staying at Anson Monroe's homestead place, over the ridge."

"I'd wanted to tell her myself, but I suppose you folks could explain it better anyway. It appears now that this Baudine and his men were indeed with that posse. According to Gordon Wilkes, they acted entirely independently and outside the authority of the posse in killing anyone. They are now wanted by the Texas Rangers and this county for the killing of Miz Bowles' husband and son."

"That's good news of a sort," Charity remarked. "What else brought you here, Sergeant?"

"This is for the two of you. Treavor Wilkes has regained consciousness and has cleared both of you of any involvement in his shooting. In fact, he claims to have a faint memory of Miss Charity here standing over him and shooting down the assassins. I, ah . . ." Sergeant Millard reached into the pouch of one saddlebag, then handed a Colt Lightning to Charity. "I brought this back to you. You dropped it in town, I believe. One last thing," he went on with a touch to his hat brim. "You both have a court appearance you must attend. It'll be mostly a formality now, but it's mandatory that you show up in Longview for the session. I hope all this has been welcome to you. If I

188

can get some water for my horse, I'll be goin' now."

"You can get a lot more than that, Sergeant," *Denili* Monroe declared. "You're welcome to stay for dinner. We've got fried ham, snap beans and baked yams."

Sergeant Millard studied the sky, the sun near the noon zenith. "How can a feller turn down an invite like that? Thank you, kindly."

An hour after the Ranger sergeant departed, Charity walked along the river bank, sent on the task of picking wild watercress for a cold chicken salad for a light supper. She made her way around the wide curve, where *Gayo'tli* and three other small Monroe boys, bare as the day they were born, splashed merrily in the water. They called to her a moment before a bullet cracked through the air from across the river.

Charity dropped like a stone.

Chapter 19

Birds took flight from the trees, their chirps of alarm shrill. Squirrels shrieked their indignation, then quickly hid from the sound they identified with sudden death. Another rifle blast split the now silent woods.

"Get down, boys," Charity called to the youngsters in the water. "Stay low and work upstream."

"Are you hurt, Charity?" *Gayo'tli* inquired in his piping voice.

"Only my dignity," she replied, her clothes, hands and face muddied. "Now hurry, get away from here."

She had only a sixgun against a rifle, or more than one, which seemed likely. She rolled from her position in the grass into the screen of a low-hanging willow. There she drew her revolver and blasted two fast shots, before moving again to another concealing position.

Gunfire erupted from two places on the opposite bank, confirming Charity's suspicion. Then, from above her, Charity heard the answering fire as Bob and *Denili* came to her aid. With them covering, she sprinted up to the level ground and dived behind a protruding rock. She immediately opened fire.

Both men had moved and their answering shots chipped stone fragments from close by Charity's face. She ducked low and reloaded. *Tsimi* and *Wili*

Monroe showed up, to take positions behind large trees and open up on the assassins. Charity used the momentary respite to study their situation.

To her left a hundred yards, a wooden bridge spanned the narrow river. Both approaches were screened by trees. With only two gunmen out there, it could be possible to flank them, she considered. That way they could be easily caught. Without consulting the others, she decided to put her plan in effect.

"Keep it up," she called out. "Pin them down."

When rapid firing began from the defenders, Charity ran a broken, zig-zag course to the barn. There she slipped a bridle on Lucifer and speedily saddled him. She turned to go out the back of the barn to find four naked, dripping wet little boys staring at her. *Gayo'tli* held out a box of cartridges.

"I brought you these," he said solemnly.

Charity produced a smile. She noticed the ammunition box indicated .44-40 cartridges. "That's thoughtful, *Gayo'tli*, but my sixgun's a thirty-eight Colt and my rifle a forty-five-sixty. You're a brave boy, all of you are, and I appreciate your efforts. Now, stay right here in the barn until this is all over."

She led Lucifer from the barn, signaled Butch to follow and mounted up. Charity rounded the barn at a gallop and streaked for the bridge. Nearing the closer approach, she freed her Marlin Pacific and chambered a round. To her sudden shock, she discovered that there had been three assassins.

The third man rose from his position covering the bridge and fired two fast shots, then pitched a thick bundle of greasy red sticks toward the center of the span. Orange sparks sputtered from the stubby fuse.

Fighting the instinct to pull up, to throw herself from the saddle, Charity charged out onto the plank floor of the bridge. In seven long strides, Lucifer

191

passed over the six sticks of dynamite, and Charity noticed the shortness of the fuse. She fired at the murderous hardcase, missing from her unstable platform, and saw a gray-black streak at Lucifer's hoofs as Butch flashed past.

A wild scream came from her would-be killer as Butch launched himself and slashed vicious fangs at the man's throat. White teeth closed on his shoulder and the full weight of Butch slammed into his chest, bowling him over. Charity thundered past the writhing, howling man and dog a moment before a huge fireball singed her auburn ponytail and Lucifer's rump. A deafening roar accompanied it, in the shape of a rolling, buffeting shock wave that nearly unseated her.

"Easy," she soothed Lucifer. "Easy, boy. Whoah, now, whoah-up."

She recovered control of the big gelding with difficulty. Even with a tight rein and soothing hand to his neck, the disturbed animal wanted to break stride and curvette across the meadow through which Charity rode him. With gentling words, she directed him in a circle that took her in behind the other assassins, as they broke from the river bank and ran for their horses. Charity's Marlin blazed three times, with only a single minor hit, which gouged flesh from one outlaw's ribs. With a running start, they broke away from her.

At once, Charity scabbarded her long gun and broke Lucifer into a gallop. A good seventy yards separated her from her quarry. Foam formed at the corners of Lucifer's mouth and whipped away in the wind. He grunted and snorted protest, skin still given to nervous twitches in reaction to the explosion. Slowly the lead enjoyed by the assassins narrowed. Lucifer paid a terrible toll for it. His energy visibly had flagged when Charity drew her Colt Lightning.

Her first shots went wild. Then, with the distance reduced to thirty yards, she reined in and took careful aim. Ahead, one of the outlaws slumped forward onto his mount's neck when a .38 Long Colt slug slammed into his back. He came only partly upright when a second bullet plowed into him. His panicked horse carried the dead man a short distance before the body fell heavily to the ground. Charity drew her second sixgun, to replace the empty one, and fired at the remaining man before she started after him.

She heard a wild cry of pain and his hat went flying. The hardcase wavered slightly in the saddle before he disappeared over a swell in the ground. Charity caught up to the dislodged hat and recognized it as belonging to Concho Bill Baudine. Anger and the desire to finish him swelled in her, to be diminished by a hail of gunfire from the far side of the ridge. Outgunned and in a vulnerable position, she had no choice but to turn around and ride away.

Charity walked Lucifer back to the Monroe farm. Once safely out of range of Baudine's men, she had halted and discovered a large splinter from the bridge stuck in Lucifer's rump. At least that explained his unusual behavior. There was little she could do out in the woods, so she eased his suffering by walking. Despite the powerful blast the bridge still stood, she discovered on her return. *Gayo'tli*, now dressed, stood at the far side to warn people off.

"You can still walk across it," he informed Charity, "but it won't take the weight of a horse. You'll have to use the ford. I'll come with you. *Agilugi* can watch the bridge," he concluded, calling for his sister.

In the farmyard, Charity asked for liniment, a sharp knife and some towels. Bob brought all three, along with a scolding.

"That was a dumb thing to do," he began. "You had me worried sick."

"I can take care of myself, Bob," Charity answered hotly. "I thought I saw a way to get to them. If I'd said anything they'd have heard and it wouldn't have worked."

"It nearly didn't," Bob snapped.

"Well, I did well enough. Now I've got two bounties lying out there that are going to decompose in this hot weather if we don't do something fast."

"Like what?" Bob, still goaded by his concern into being snappish, demanded.

"Take them in to Longview."

"What! Gordon Wilkes still has a price on your head. You wouldn't stand a chance."

"You can come along, if you want. Anyone else for that matter. First let me get this splinter out of Lucifer's rump."

"What's this about you goin' into town?" Evan Monroe inquired, striking across the yard from the house. He and the rest of his sons had come at the sound of gunfire.

"I'm going to turn in two of Bill Baudine's men for the bounty," Charity declared flatly, while she washed the area of Lucifer's wound with liniment.

"Me an' my boys'll escort you then," Evan offered.

"All *five* of them?" Charity asked.

"Sure enough," Evan assured her, reaching out to ruffle *Gayo'tli*'s mop of hair. "*Gayo'tli* is a good shot, even if he's a runt."

"Maybe the women folk should come too," Bob suggested only half seriously.

"Why not?" Evan agreed. "We've been hidin' away

194

too damned long."

"I think I've started something," Charity observed as she took up the knife.

Carefully she made an incision along the length of the sliver and pulled the lips apart with her strong fingers. Lucifer flinched and nickered.

"Hold his head Bob," Charity ordered. She cut again, deeper.

Charity released the knife and used both hands to open the incision and work free the shard of wood. Lucifer snorted and stamped his hoofs. Bob hung on tightly to keep the powerful gelding from tossing his large, anvil head. With a soft sucking sound the offending particle came free.

"That's got it. Hand me that salve."

Deftly Charity packed and covered the wound and put away the implements. She located some broken bits of horehound candy in a saddle bag and rewarded her patient for enduring the operation so well. Shoe-button eyes looked up with bright eagerness at Charity.

"What about me?" *Gayo'tli* asked.

Charity handed him a piece of the sweet amid the adults' laughter.

Gordon Wilkes had barely returned from a visit to the hospital in Nacogdoches when one of his hands arrived, hat in hand. "Some of Baudine's men took a few shots at that Charity Rose, up at the Monroe farm," the squint-eyed rider informed his boss.

Mention of Baudine's name caused old Gordon to burn. Even knowing that his grandson lived, after being lied to by Baudine, wasn't enough to temper his anger. This mess with the Carrolls, that woman, his grandson, and Baudine's high-handed ways made his life more than a little crowded.

"What happened?" Gordon demanded.

"They tried to shoot her from ambush. She killed two of them and wounded Baudine slightly."

"Damned shame she didn't get them all."

"I thought you had a price on her?" the cowhand remarked.

"I do. That grandson of mine's workin' on me to lift it. He insists she had nothing to do with the shooting. Well, I'll tell you this. If she hadn't come to him to help Bob Carroll, Treavor would never have been shot."

"You're a mighty hard man, Mister Wilkes," the hand observed.

"Yep. And stubborn, too."

"Ouch!" Bill Baudine exclaimed. "Goddamnit, Frenchy, are you trying to squeeze my lungs out through my mouth?"

"It's a deep gouge, *mon ami*, and it bleeds easily. If you want it to stop, before you leak to death, the bandage must be tight, *non?*"

"The thing is," Bill started off on a new tack, "now we're on everybody's list. What are we goin' to do about that?"

"It is, perhaps, time to take up what we've made and return to New Mexico, eh?"

"Naw, Frenchy, it's not time for that. We need to get a great deal more. Sooner or later that feud will hot up again. When it does, we can line our pockets by hitting both sides."

"You disremember the Texas Rangers are after us, too? Where will we hide?" Frenchy asked, concern evident in his tone.

"There'll be somewhere. Hell, if nothin' else,

196

there's caves in those hills to the north. We could hole up there a while, then hit wherever it pleases us."

"What about Charity Rose, Bill? Do we forget about that—that vile woman?"

Concho Bill shivered. "The mention of her name chills me," he admitted. "I won't rest until I know she's dead."

Frenchy began putting away the medical supplies. "Do you have any ideas on how to go about making her dead?"

"I wish I did. The longer she's out there, poking around, the greater our risk. What do you think, Frenchy?"

"I suggest that we poison her, *mon ami.*"

"*Poison?* How? Who could get close enough to her?"

Frenchy flashed a cold, sardonic smile. "That could be arranged. She and the Monroe family, and that Bob Carroll, went into Longview to collect the rewards on our men. She will be staying at the Republic House, as usual." Frenchy paused a moment, outlining the plan. "A little accident, a vacancy in the hotel kitchen or dining staff, and *voila!* She is no more."

Baudine's eyes narrowed, "That's a grisly way of going about it."

"*Oui,* but effective."

"If I thought you were serious . . ." Baudine's hand slid to the polished grips of his sixgun. "Shit, I've never even poisoned a water hole during a range war. There are some things that . . . just stick in a feller's craw. Forget it, Frenchy. Her time will come."

Chapter 20

Longview seemed calm enough when the little cavalcade arrived. People went about their business with a relaxed air. The ring of hammer and anvil came from the blacksmithy and smoke belched from the forge. The corpses had been wrapped in India rubber ground cloths and brought in a wagon. The Monroes dropped off at the Republic House and the harness shop, leaving Charity and Bob alone to pay a visit on Sheriff Hogan.

"What do we have here?" he asked uneasily as the buckboard rolled to a stop.

"I brought you two wanted men, Sheriff. I'd appreciate if you'd check them over and put in the authorization for my reward. They were members of the Bill Baudine gang."

"How'd they meet their end?" Hogan asked tightly.

"My dog got one and I shot the other," Charity told him simply.

Hogan winced. "What were they doing to get themselves killed?"

"The one I shot had been popping a few rounds at me. The other one threw a bundle of dynamite at my horse and I."

Hogan shook his head sadly. "You play rough

games. You know that Gordon Wiles put a price on your head, Miss Charity?"

"Yes, I'm well aware of it. That's part of why I'm here. I want to go into court and get this all straightened out. By now he must know neither Bob nor I had anything to do with shooting his grandson. I want to face him in public and get the facts out."

"You'll be hard pressed to do that," the sheriff advised.

"Why's that? Once I talk to Treavor, I'm sure he'll see to it his grandfather listens."

"Young Wilkes isn't here any more, Miss Charity," Hogan told her. "He went back to Nacogdoches to recuperate."

"I'll have to write him, then, or go there," Charity suggested.

"The first will take too long and I don't think you'd live through the second," Sheriff Hogan argued. "I've got a way, though, that might do."

"What's that?" Charity inquired.

"Call him on my telephone."

"Why, I . . . I've never used one of them before."

"High time you did, then. Come on in, I'll have Doc Trowbridge take care of the dead men and you can make a call to Nacogdoches."

Inside, Charity gingerly handled the unfamiliar device after Sheriff Hogan had vigorously turned the crank and yelled into the little grille, instructing someone unseen to connect them through to Nacogdoches. At the sheriff's urging, she put the instrument to her ear.

A crackle of static came at her, along with a hollow surging like the rush of excited blood over an ear drum. She took it away, questioningly, then put it back. A weak, tinny voice spoke to her ear.

"Hello, Central? Is this Nacogdoches Central?"

"Hello? Who's calling?"

"This is Ida at Longview Central. Is this Nacogdoches?"

"Oh, for goodness sakes, Ida. Of course it is. This is Tilly."

"Ring up Doc Meyer's hospital for me, Tilly. I got a call for young Treavor Wilkes."

"Who's calling, Ida?"

"I don't know as yet. It's from the sheriff's office."

"Oh. I'll put you right through."

More clicks, scratches and crackles came. Then a man's voice. "Doc Meyer. Hello? Hello? Confounded thing. *Hello!*"

"Doc, this is Ida up Longview way. Can your patient come to the telephone?"

"Which one?" came the physician's cranky retort.

"Treavor Wilkes," Ida responded.

"Well, why didn't you say so? Hello? Hello? Are you still there?"

"I'm still here, Doc. Get Treavor Wilkes to the telephone."

A long minute passed and then Charity heard, barely recognizable, the voice of Treavor Wilkes. "Hello? Anyone there?"

Looking confounded, Charity turned a stricken face to Sheriff Hogan. "What do I do?"

"Talk into that thing you've got to your ear," the lawman instructed.

"Then how can I hear him?"

"Put it back, of course."

Dubious, Charity held the black, conical object in front of her face. "Treavor . . . is that you, Treavor?"

A weak squawking rattled the diaphragm of the telephone handset.

"Put it to your ear," Hogan snapped.

"—ow who's there?" Treavor queried.

Slowly Charity mastered the odd mechanics of the instrument. She took it from her head again and spoke. "This is Charity Rose. Are you there, Treavor?"

Back in place, she heard his tinny voice. "Sure I'm here. Where are you?"

"In Longview, at the sheriff's office," Ida's voice came on the line, impatient.

"I'm in Longview at the sheriff's office," Charity informed him when she had the speaker grille in front of her face.

"Hello? I'm getting an echo," Treavor remarked. "What are you doing there?"

"I brought in two of Baudine's men for the bounty. They attacked us out at the Monroe farm. Are you all right?"

"What kind of a lady goes around shooting people?" Tilly injected gratuitously. "I'd watch my P's and Q's, Treavor Wilkes, I would."

"I'm all right, Charity. It's you I'm worried about. My grandfather doesn't seem to want to believe me. You should have stayed where you were safe."

"If you call getting shot at by Baudine's hardcases being safe, then we'd still be back at the farm."

"Hello? Did you say you were going back to the farm? Don't. Stay in town, now you're there. Preferably in the jail, in protective custody. I'm sure Matt Hogan would do that for you. Then stay tight until I get there. I'll take the next stage."

"I'm not going to be locked up in a jail. Not even as a *guest*," Charity snapped back. "We'll stay at the Republic House."

Treavor groaned. "Are you feelin' poorly, Treavor?" Tilly inquired solicitously. Treavor groaned again.

"Charity, listen to me. You should never have used

201

the telephone to reach me. Goddamnit," he fumed, "don't you know that everyone on the line knows where you are right now?"

"No," Charity's hesitant reply came to him. "I'm a stranger to the workings of this new-fangled contraption."

"Take my word for it. There's two operators and who knows how many more people who have heard what you plan to do. That could get you killed before I can change my granddad's mind."

"I—I'm sorry, Treavor. But, to me it doesn't make any difference. I'm tired of waiting around and getting shot at by surprise. Let 'em come and do their worst. At least then I can see their faces."

"Charity, Charity, you're hopeless but I love you for it. I'll come right away. Good-bye."

"Uh . . . oh, er, good-bye, Treavor."

Shaking with ill-concealed laughter Sheriff Hogan pointed to the square white oak box with two bells and a hook that hung on the wall, connected to the handset by a cloth-covered wire. "You can hang it up now," he informed her.

Still ruffled by Treavor's lecture, Charity stomped from the office, giving back a clipped thank you. Bob followed her and they entered the Republic House bar. Its plush, dim-lighted interior boasted far more luxury than the regular saloons of the town, with crystal chandeliers and a huge, beveled glass mirror behind the mahogany. Brass twinkled and muted conversation made a soft, surf-like intrusion on the air redolent with the odor of lemons, bitters and malty beer.

"After that, I need a drink," Charity announced, startling Bob, who'd seen her take only a little wine with meals.

"What would you have?" he asked, working to take

it in stride.

"A Sazerac cocktail sounds nice."

Charity looked around the room, recognizing a number of the hill folk who must have been entering town since they arrived at the sheriff's office. The townmen who occupied tables or space at the bar eyed them with visible unease, noting the prevalence of firearms among the silent, closed-faced people.

"A, ah, gathering of the clans?" Charity asked of Bob.

"You might say that. Everyone wants to be certain you're still alive when Treavor gets here. After that, it's in the hands of the judge."

By early morning, supporters of both sides had thronged into Longview. The streets became congested and the locals began to fear for the safety of their lives and property. Stray bullets, they knew, cared nothing about innocent bystanders. When the stage from Nacogdoches arrived, an electric tension crackled along Main Street.

Charity Rose met the eleven o'clock coach, along with Bob Carroll, and the Monroes. All were armed and watchful. Charity's unease grew when the vehicle rolled to a stop outside the Wells Fargo office. Three grim-faced men rode on top, along with the driver and shotgun. All bristled with weapons. The door opened slowly and a hard-visaged quartet emerged, rifles in hand. The crowd of on-lookers grew deathly silent and shrank back. Then Treavor Wilkes stepped out, moving slowly because of the tenderness of his wound.

Murmured remarks rippled through the watchers. Their exclamations rose in alarmed consternation when the final passenger came from the coach.

Blinking in the bright sunlight, Gordon Wilkes placed his hat squarely on his big, shaggy head and glanced around at the reception committee. His flinty blue eyes fixed on Charity Rose.

"You're Charity Rose," a statement not a question, growled in Gordon Wilkes' familiar manner.

"I am." Charity fought the inclination to draw and fire before the others could react.

"My grandson said you'd be here to greet us. Good! Now we can take care of it all at once."

Once more the crowd drew away from the center of danger. Gordon Wilkes' hard, lined features softened into a big smile as he turned slowly to take in all who had assembled. He raised one huge, slab-muscled arm for silence.

"I'm here to lift the reward I mistakenly placed on this woman in the county where I executed it. She is not to be harmed. If anyone disobeys that directive, they'll answer to me. While I'm at it, I'm going to have all charges dropped against young Robert here and any of the rest of you who have been involved of late."

Too shocked to react, the crowd stared, gape-mouthed. Again Gordon Wilkes searched the faces close at hand. Too vain to wear the glasses he should, Wilkes would never admit to his near-sightedness. When he ascertained that the person he sought was not there, he directed his question to Charity and Bob.

"Where's Bentbow Carroll?"

"He's not here, Mister Wilkes," Bob answered.

"Well, somebody ought to bring him. I've come to make my peace with him and all of you. There's been too damn much killin' and about half of that done on account of lies told to me by a scoundrel worse than any stubborn Carroll or Monroe. So I've come to make up. Eh? There anyone here again' that?"

At last the tide of tension broke in a mighty roar of approval. Men shouted and stamped, whistled and slapped others on the back. Wilkes' advocates rushed to embrace Carroll supporters and vice-versa. Gordon Wilkes shook Bob Carroll's hand, under the watchful protection of the men he had brought along. Eyes twinkling, he then bent to kiss Charity on the cheek.

"If I was twenty years younger, you'd have a problem, Missy," he told her. "Now," he informed those closest to the scene, "let's go down to the Republic and have a drink."

In a tumult of happy voices, the Carroll-Wilkes feud ended. Half a block away, in the doorway to his office, Sheriff Matt Hogan rested his hand on the butt-stock of his sixgun and shook his head in wonder. He'd have to hurry, he goaded himself, if he wanted to get in on the drinks.

Chapter 21

WANTED   WANTED
DEAD OR ALIVE
A Committee of Responsible Citizens
from Harrison and Nacogdoches Counties,
Texas will pay for the apprehension, DEAD or
ALIVE of WILLIAM BAUDINE, aka Concho
Bill Baudine
a REWARD of $2,000
and an additional $1,000 each for the members
of his gang named below:
Maurice "Frenchy" Descoines
Norbert "Bert" Clay
Ezekial Walton
Isaac Tremble and John Does 1 - 20
To claim reward, send proof to:
Sheriff Matthew Hogan, Longview, Texas.
REWARD WILL BE PAID DEAD OR ALIVE

For Gordon Wilkes and the Carroll's the feud
might be over. But for Concho Bill Baudine, his
gang, and Dermott Wilkes, the looting and carnage
was not. The word of the meeting between faction
leaders spread rapidly and plans began for a huge
celebration in Longview, followed by one in

Nacogdoches. One thing the hill people of both Scottish and Cherokee origin knew how to do was lay on a party. While preparations went forward, Concho Bill and Dermott met to reorganize their designs.

"Granddad's lost his mind. He's gone soft," Dermott Wilkes declared in an angry tone. "He's even turned on you."

"It isn't the first time," Concho Bill assured him. "Quite often, someone hires our sort of, ah, services, only to turn moral and churchy and set the law on us for doing our job."

"You take it all so philosophically," Dermott observed.

"I take it realistically," Bill responded. "Ours is not an easy life. It never has been. What we want now is to gather all the loot and loose cash we can and be on our way."

"Implying what?" Dermott queried.

Concho Bill produced a "V" shaped, wolfish smile. "While everyone is up at Longview celebrating, it's an ideal time to help ourselves to whatever is lying around this part of the country. Including a couple of banks."

"That's out of the question. It would seriously harm the family holdings."

"Are you so concerned over that? Your cousin joined the other side, and has now convinced your grandfather to end the feud. Are you really so protective of what he would inherit? Why not take yours now and leave with us?"

A cold light glowed in Dermott's watery eyes. "You've a point there, Bill. I am the one who hired you."

"Yes, and your grandfather fired us, set the law on us. To me, that's an open invitation to pay-back time. Do you think for a minute that all will be as

207

before between you and him? How else are you going to profit from this?" Bill's voice became smooth and persuasive. "Think it through, Dermott. It won't take long for your grandfather to remember who first brought us into this. Do you think he'll thank you for it?"

"All right, then," Dermott relented. "We—we'll do it. What places do you plan on hitting?"

"Gordon Wilkes', of course, to add insult to injury," Concho Bill began without hesitation. Quickly he laid out the rest of his proposed raids.

Miles Tanner had been a teamster for the Wilkes family for fifteen years. He did rather well at it. Enough so that he was able to purchase six tandem rigged Conestoga freighters and hire drivers. His business prospered. Tanner rarely took out a load any more, so he sat in the office of his freight line when three men burst through the door.

"Hand over the cash box and open that safe," the nattily dressed one in the middle demanded. Tanner recognized a faint New Orleans French accent.

"What the hell do you think you're doin'?" Miles growled.

"Make it fast or I'll put a bullet in you," Frenchy Descoines came back.

Tanner produced the cash box from a drawer of his desk and rose to go to the safe. Another of the bandits gave him a violent shove and his teamster's temper flared. With a blinding fast spin, he launched a ham-like fist at his tormentor. He felt bone give in the man's jaw while the familiar ache and lightning shock of collapsed knuckles radiated up his arm.

New pain followed it as he found himself sucking on the muzzle of Frenchy's sixgun. "I ought to blow

208

your head off, *couchon,* but I need you to open the safe. Get at it," Frenchy hissed.

Thoughts of his five tow-headed youngsters, the eldest only twelve, sped through Tanner's mind. He nodded gingerly and made signs that he would cooperate. Five minutes later, Frenchy and his companions rode away from Miles High Freight with three thousand dollars. They left a bleeding, dying Miles Tanner behind.

Down in a draw they located the mixing sheds where water and raw alcohol were blended. Seven workmen kept busy at their usual tasks. Twelve of Baudine's men rode in shouting, firing their revolvers. Taken by surprise, the workers threw up their hands and stood aside. It being payday, eight hundred dollars waited in the money drawer. Laughing and shouting, the outlaws rode off.

One woman in the Appleby bank, a retired school teacher, screamed in fright when five masked men entered, weapons at the ready. The other customers raised their hands and backed against the wall without need of the shouted instructions.

"Line up over there!"

"This is a stickup!"

"Nobody make any sudden moves."

The faceless men went quickly to their tasks. The three who had spoken watched the customers and relieved them of their money, while the other pair went behind the tellers' cages and scooped up the bank's assets. Pennies and other small coin clattered on the floor. The schoolmarm made weak sobbing noises and wobbled on the edge of a faint.

"Now," the apparent leader commanded when the robbery had been completed, "we want you all to stay nice and quiet and inside here for five minutes. That way no one will be hurt. We're leavin' a man outside to make sure you do as you're told. Thanks, folks, for the donation."

Two minutes passed before the bank president, trembling more from anger and indignation than fear, took a nickel plated, pearl handled revolver from the top drawer of his desk and walked through the front door. A moment's silence followed, then the crack of a rifle sounded from the second floor of the hotel and the banker fell dead on the boardwalk.

A large round dance had started in the principal intersection of Longview, Texas. Wilkes men danced with Carroll ladies, the Carroll young blades sought Wilkes girls. A large band played and beer flowed freely from open-topped kegs, set on trestle tables. Bob Carroll, with Charity at his side and Treavor Wilkes right on hand, held court over the festivities. While they did, Gordon Wilkes matched Bentbow Carroll cup for cup of the "best sippin' rum west of Barbados."

The mellow, twenty-year old product of the Carroll distillery was duly pronounced drinkable by men of stout heart and five barrels rolled out to fuel the jubilation. Steers, hogs and goats roasted on huge barbecue pits. Into this scene of joyful reconciliation strode a grim-faced man who approached Bob Carroll and removed his hat.

"Bob, Treavor, I've got some bad news."

"Not at a time like this, Loren," Bob told Loren Vale.

" 'Fraid so, Bob. It's more vexin' to Treavor, I

210

reckon. That bunch your cousin hired, Baudine and his longriders? Well, they've took to raiding down Nacogdoches way. Killed some folks, despoiled some ladies, ah, yer pardon, ma'am," Loren acknowledged Charity. "Robbed banks and stuck up stages."

"Damnit!" Treavor exploded. "We've have to do something about it and fast. I'll gather some men."

"So will I," Bob offered.

"I'm coming along," Charity informed them. "I want Baudine for myself."

Bob frowned. He harbored secret visions of a wedding, a nice sized farm and auburn-haired kiddies running around. "It's likely to be dangerous."

"I'm used to that. And I won't be argued out of it. Give me fifteen minutes."

Half an hour later, with the party still in full bloom, a sizable group of Wilkes men, Carrolls, Monroes and Charity Rose, departed from Longview. Loren Vale offered to guide them to where Sheriff Frazer McCall and a posse trailed the gang from their latest attack.

Frazer McCall had no choice but to split his posse. He left two men at the rendezvous point to inform anyone coming to his aid what had happened. They hailed the posse from Longview late in the afternoon of the following day. When everyone had gathered in close, the deputies explained the situation.

"Sheriff McCall and half of the men went on after the original group. Some of the outlaws split off here and the sheriff suspected they might be set to double back and hit some other places. He sent the undersheriff and the rest after them," the senior of the pair reported.

"I'm inclined to agree," Bob Carroll remarked. "In

which case, maybe we should go after those who broke off."

"They'll eventually lead us to the others," Charity offered. "If they're up to no good, maybe we can catch up before they have the chance."

"We'll leave one man here, and one of you come along," Treavor suggested.

"Sounds good," the senior deputy agreed. "Ed you go along with these folks. Make it sort of official that way."

Ed Cotter fetched his horse and swung into the saddle. "Beats sittin' here on my butt for days on end," he opined.

"Where would be the nearest target of value?" Charity asked.

"Ummmm. I'd say the bank in Sacul," Ed Cotter advised.

"Then that's where we'll head," Charity spoke assuredly.

Glass flew outward in big shards from the front window of the Farmers' Mutual Bank in Sacul, followed instantly by the report of a .45 revolver. A woman's scream, and angry voices sounded next.

"We said for nobody to play hero," an angry snarl rasped out.

"Next one of you gets smart, we kill everyone," Wes Noonan drawled.

"Get busy, old man," Frenchy Descoines barked at a teller.

"I'm movin' fast as I can," the elderly clerk complained.

Grinning, Frenchy produced a knife and held it close to the wattled skin of the teller's neck. "Perhaps I can induce you to work faster, *mais non?*"

At the edge of town seven of McCall's posse reined in. They had followed the group that had split off since the previous day. The outlaws had stolen fresh horses, their pursuers had no opportunity to replace flagging mounts. Their number, too, seemed insignificant against the ruthless horde they proposed to corral. The leader, Under-Sheriff Davey Clayborne, spoke to that effect.

"There's too many of them for us to take on face to face. And no way of telling which way they'll head from here. So an ambush is out. What we need to do is wait for night and hit them in their camp."

"If they stop overnight," a posseman advised.

"I wouldn't worry about takin' 'em at the bank now, Davey," another volunteer deputy drawled softly. "We got company an' it looks like they came to help." His nod indicated the road beyond them and a group of horsemen approaching along it.

"If we got that lucky, we'd be fools not to take advantage," Davey observed. "One of you go find out who that is."

When the under-sheriff learned that the posse had come from Longview he began to lay out a plan to trap Baudine's men in the bank. They'd all better hurry, he admonished the newcomers, the bandits had been inside for five minutes already. Breaking into smaller groups, the reinforced posse moved in.

Only a fraction of a second after the lawmen reached their designated positions, two of the outlaws stepped out of the bank and hurried to where another held the horses. The trio mounted and kept watch on the street. Right then, at the worst possible time, an over-anxious civilian posseman lost control and opened fire.

Others immediately took up firing. Bullets hummed and cracked and cleared all three from their mounts. Return shots came from within the bank. Women began to scream and Under-Sheriff Clayborne at last shouted loud enough to get a cease fire.

"We've got ten people in here, including three women," a voice called from the bank. "We'll kill them all if you don't back off and let us out of here."

"We have you surrounded," Davey Clayborne shouted back, the words seeming foolish even to him. "Leave those folks unharmed and you might not hang."

A dry, cynical chuckle answered him. "We won't hang. If you don't let us out, we'll die fighting, after we kill a lot of you and the hostages."

"Who's in charge there?" Charity Rose called out.

"I am," a French-accented voice responded. "That must be M'amselle Charity Rose, *n'est pas?*"

"Frenchy, this is no bluff. The bank is surrounded. Give up and you have a chance."

"*Mais oui,* and pigs wear pajamas."

A hail of lead came from the bank. Worried over the hostages, Davey Clayborne ordered everyone not to fire except at a clear target. After several minutes the firing dwindled. Tense and watchful, the posse started forward.

"It's okay," a voice came from inside the bank. "They've gone."

"How?" Davey asked rhetorically. "We'd have heard something."

"I have a feeling whomever you sent around back ran into some trouble," Charity suggested.

A quick check proved her right. Four men lay dead in the alley. None of them were outlaws.

For the next three days, the two posses made wide, sweeping searches of the area, uncovering only cold trails and abandoned camps. Even with refreshed mounts the stamina of the searchers waned rapidly. Many had farms or businesses to attend to. Few could spare more than another day. At last, with only a handful, Charity Rose, Bob Carroll, the Monroe boys and five men with Under-Sheriff Clayborne set out on the last likely trail. Restless, Charity scouted ahead with young Henry Monroe.

Over a period of two hours they maintained a steady two mile lead on the posse. Charity had about decided they were chasing shadows when a fresh-broken branch on a hickory caught her attention. She whistled sharply, in imitation of a cardinal and Henry came to her side.

"Look at that," she said quietly.

"Not an hour old, I'd guess," Henry pronounced.

"It's so moist here, I'd have figured longer. I'll go back and bring the others. Keep after the sign."

"Ummm. I'll mark the way while I go."

Twenty minutes later the posse reached the spot. Charity urged them on at a gallop and soon they topped a rise. Below, tails of the last horses disappearing into the woods beyond a clearing, they spotted the gang. At once the chase heated up. A determined run put the posse in sight of the fleeing outlaws.

Hastily seen signs indicated the entire band had joined together in the meadow. Now they fled in confusion before a force of only half their size. Charity estimated they must be low on ammunition and heavy with loot to choose flight over fight. In minutes they came within rifle range.

A few shots from the pursuers put the gang into headlong retreat. Twisting and turning among the rocks and hills, Concho Bill led his gang away from the relentless followers. Unfamiliar with the terrain,

Baudine took a wrong turn and found much too late he had ridden into a steep, narrow canyon, formed by a small, fast-flowing stream. At the far end, a thin ribbon of waterfall cascaded from the higher ground beyond, through a rock-strewn defile. Cornered, they turned to give fight.

Chapter 22

Birds started from their perches and the musical tinkle of the waterfall disappeared under a blazing rattle of gunfire. The posse scattered in search of protection behind rocks and trees and began a slow, hazardous advance. Charity Rose, *Tsimi* Monroe and Bob Carroll held the center, blocking the trail. Movement ahead of them gave Charity a target.

Her first slug cut out the reins of Zeke Walton's mount and the second slammed into his right side. He uttered a soft groan and fell off into a cluster of small boulders. She turned in search of another outlaw when Bert Clay opened up from the notch of a tree.

Hot lead struck the dirt close in front of Charity's face and sent her rolling behind a large, mossy rock. Clay fired again and a soft grunt came from *Tsimi* Monroe. Charity crawled to his side and located a bullet hole in the top of his right shoulder, behind the collar bone.

"Got my lung," he said calmly, a slight gurgle in his voice. "I can hold on."

"You should pull back," Charity suggested.

"No. I'll be all right."

Charity turned her attention to the outlaws, who scrambled among the rocks, firing if they saw even the faintest scrap of target. She chipped shards of stone that set a brigand to howling, pawing at his face as he walked out into a blizzard of lead that cut him to shreds. Charity picked another indistinct target and squeezed off a round as she heard a hollow *whop-whop* beside her.

A quick glance down informed her that both bullets had entered the top of *Tsimi*'s head. He lay still in a pool of blood. She had not yet placed Bert Clay in the tree and searched among the boulders for the sniper. Another close-cracking shot that tore fur from Butch's forepaw and brought a whine from the half-wolf betrayed Clay's position. Charity squirmed away from the vulnerable position and retrieved her Marlin Pacific from the saddle scabbard.

Mind fixed on the smudge of smoke in the big oak, she sighted in and squeezed off a round. Leaves trembled and fell, then a body came into view.

"Yaaaaaiiiii!" Bert Clay shrieked as he fell thirty feet, head-first onto the rocks. It saved him the slow agony of death from the gut shot Charity had given him.

Three of the Monroes came to their feet and rushed forward. For a long moment gunfire pinned them down only ten yards from their starting point. Then the Carrolls started a heavy volley and the two teams rushed to the foot of the knoll on which the gang concentrated their defenses.

"They're gettin' too damned close," Ike Tremble observed over the bark of gunfire.

"We'd better pull back," Ollie Bates suggested.

218

"To where?" Concho Bill asked sarcastically.

"I took a look at that waterfall. If we could delay the posse, we might have a chance to climb up alongside it and get away," Bates explained.

Concho Bill considered the possibility. "I've got some dynamite in my pack saddle. It's wrapped careful, but watch how you handle it. Bring it here and we'll see what we can do."

Bates returned in three minutes with half a dozen fused and capped sticks. Concho Bill looked at them lovingly. "All right. Go get the rest. When I say so, start laying down some heavy fire. I'll throw the sticks and we'll pull back to the falls."

Bob Carroll came to his feet and ran forward as the outlaws blazed away wildly to cover their leader. He saw the first stick arc through the late afternoon sky, sparks spouting from a short length of fuse, a moment before a sledge hammer blow struck his right thigh. Force of the impact spun him around and he went down a moment before the dynamite exploded.

A bright flash of orange light, with ear-shattering blast and a huge ball of dust rose from among the rocks. Dislodged, half a dozen stones, from fist size to that of a small dog, began to roll downhill. The outlaws' firing grew in volume and another stick flew toward the attacking posse.

"Get back!" Davey Clayborne shouted. "Dynamite. Get back."

Blast followed blast. Fearful for their lives, the possemen drew away. Smoke, acrid fumes and billowing dust blocked the view. Charity took a quick look around.

"Where's Bob?" she asked, fearful of the answer.

219

"Didn't see him," Clayborne responded. "I think he took a hit out there."

"We've got to go after him," Charity urged.

"Not with that dynamite goin' off."

"You can come along, Sheriff, or stay. *I'm* going."

"Wait now, Miss Charity . . ." Clayborne called as her slim figure disappeared into the swirling miasma.

Rubble blocked the trail and game paths and, under cover of the dust and smoke, the remainder of the gang pulled back. Concho Bill held back three sticks of dynamite for emergency use. With his best shots as rear guard, he started some of the men up the irregular, eroded chimney that paralleled the waterfall. From down the canyon they heard the sounds of reorganization.

"Let's get after them," *Denili* Monroe hollered.

"Where's Bob?" Charity's voice could be heard. Several moments passed, then Charity called out. "Over here. I've found him. I need help."

Concho Bill produced a thin, wicked smile. He'd slowed them down. Let them tend their wounded and gather the dead. That might give him precious time. In the meanwhile, he decided to send a few random shots down the canyon to keep their heads low.

"Take a few shots down there. Don't need to aim at anything unless you see it. I want to keep them hopping."

"I think I've found a way around them," Charity told the rest at a whispered strategy meeting. "The left side of that knoll rises enough that it looks impassable, yet it's not. That's where I found Bob. I can get through and circle them. I'll take Butch and I want two of you to come with me."

"I'll go," *Denili* Monroe offered.

"Take me," his brother, Henry, appealed.

"All right. Let's do it fast," Charity ordered.

"We could wait for dark," Clayborne suggested.

"And maybe give them a chance to slip away?" Charity came back. "Not likely."

Charity and the Monroes covered three hundred yards without attracting a single shot. Prone behind the crown of a slight rise, the brothers waited while she slid forward and studied the ground beyond. Her diligence paid off when she spotted the outlaw positions, exposed and vulnerable to them at that angle. Three of four rifles from here would make it a slaughter. Quietly, careful not to raise dust, she slid back and informed the Monroes.

"Harry, you go back and tell them what we discovered. I want one more man up here and we'll open up after the rest make a frontal attack. Together we can crush them."

In five minutes the two-pronged attack had been set in place. *Tsatsi* Carroll led the charge of the posse, with Under-Sheriff Clayborne at his side. At the moment they came under fire from the defending outlaws, Charity's small band opened up.

Superior force now on the side of the law, the battle quickly closed to a hand-to-hand skirmish. Unable to fire effectively, Charity led the Monroe brothers down the slope and into the melee. Colt Lightning blazing, Charity cut down two hardcases, and ducked a swinging rifle butt. Dust rose and she sought in vain to locate Concho Bill Baudine and Frenchy Descoines. She saw Ike Tremble break off from the struggle and run back beyond the next rise.

Grimly determined to finish the gang, Charity started that way. Terrible pain registered only a fraction of a second as bright lights burst in her head and she fell forward, swirling, down, down, down, into a pool of darkness.

Charity awakened to the low murmur of voices and indistinct shapes moving around a campfire. A fire in the middle of a fight? A groan escaped her rough, dry throat as she sought to rise. Gentle pressure from a large hand eased her back onto a thick pile of saddle blankets.

"Take it easy, Charity," Bob Carroll urged. "You've been out for nearly an hour."

"Wha—why . . . ? Where's Baudine? What happened?"

"One at a time," *Denili* Monroe urged. "The fight's over. Those we didn't kill or capture escaped."

"How?"

"Climbed up beside the waterfall. Baudine and Descoines among them."

"Oh, damnit, damnit!" Charity cursed, senses reeling as she sat upright. Then she recalled Bob's wound. "Bob, how—how are you? They didn't, didn't . . ."

"No, they didn't get the job done. I'm in one piece, but mighty sore. The doc'll have to take a good look at it when we get back."

"The truth is," *Tsatsi* Carroll injected, "he's not as well off as you. Keeps driftin' off and he's lost a lot of blood. It'll take a wagon to get him to town. He's stubborn, though."

Charity's worry over Bob dimmed slightly as she looked upward at the invisible rumble of water from the fall. Baudine. She'd rest and get after him. He couldn't be allowed to get away again. Driven by the urgency of her quest she started to rise, only to have he world swirl and drift away again.

June had come to Nacogdoches by the time Char-
ty and Bob returned. Likewise, the continuing party
rom Longview. Bob's wound had been a bad one,
leep and infected by the time he reached a doctor in
Nacogdoches. Doctor Meyer probed and poked and
packed the bullet hole and after four days released
Bob from the hospital. Charity he worried over even
more. She'd taken a severe blow from a rifle butt and
he suspected her skull had been cracked. For three
days she continued to pass out unexpectedly. Her
eyes tended not to focus and she complained of
dizziness. Troubled by tremendous headaches she
would cry out in sleep or unconsciousness, turn
restlessly and then sink into a near coma.

Her head remained bandaged when the couple set
out from the small hospital to the hotel. Bob had
recovered sufficiently to be anxious to get in on the
celebration. The Mexican population of Nacogdoches had joined the festive spirit with their
special dishes and Bob wanted to dig in to the
elbows. For love of Charity, he waited through two
days of fiesta, until she seemed steady enough to
participate. Eagerly he called at her room.

"I do want to go, Bob," Charity protested. "Yet,
'm still a little unsure on my feet."

"You're feeling good enough to be up and
dressed," Bob protested. "Have been for three days
now. We don't have to dance the *fandango* or anything, just get in on some of the fun and the eating.
We're guests of honor, after all. Everyone's excited
about the Baudine gang being run out of the coun-
ry."

Charity's frown stopped his bubbling enthusiasm.

223

"That's what's got me, Bob. They got away. I wante[d] them so bad. I should be on their trail now."

Slowly she unwound her turban of bandage. [A] deep sigh raised and lowered her pert breasts. "Yo[u] know, with that thing off it doesn't hurt nearly s[o] much. I think I might be able to go out for a whil[e] after all."

Bob stood as one stricken. He had been filled wit[h] a different sort of excitement, only to be captivate[d] by the lovely lines of Charity's exquisite body as sh[e] moved before the mirror of her dressing table. Th[e] breath stuck in his throat and he took hesitant step[s] forward, arms out, to be slipped around her fro[m] behind.

Instantly jolted with her own injury-suppresse[d] desire, Charity vibrated with an flaring bolt of pa[s]sion. A wide, sweet smile spread on her face and he[r] eyes glowed with welcoming ardor as Bob's hand[s] cupped and squeezed her breasts.

"Oh, Bob, Bob. Make love to me right now, the[n] again, and again, and I'll let you take me to all th[e] parties you want," she exclaimed breathlessly.

For now at least, for some while to come, sh[e] relented, Concho Bill Baudine could wait for his ju[st] desserts.